The Runaway Jury

JOHN GRISHAM

Level 6

Retold by Hilary Maxwell-Hyslop
Series Editors: Andy Hopkins and Jocelyn Potter

Pearson Education Limited
Edinburgh Gate, Harlow,
Essex CM20 2JE, England
and Associated Companies throughout the world.

ISBN: 978-1-4058-8270-5

First published by Arrow Books 1997
New edition first published by Penguin Books Ltd 2001
This edition first published 2008

1 3 5 7 9 10 8 6 4 2

Typeset by Graphicraft Ltd, Hong Kong
Set in 11/14pt Bembo
Printed in China
SWTC/01

Published by Pearson Education Ltd in association with
Penguin Books Ltd, both companies being subsidiaries of Pearson Plc

For a complete list of the titles available in the Penguin Readers series please write to your local ·
Pearson Longman office or to: Penguin Readers Marketing Department, Pearson Education,
Edinburgh Gate, Harlow, Essex CM20 2JE, England.

Contents

Introduction

Behind the lawyers sat the jury consultants, watching the possible jurors for any gestures—arms folded across the chest, or fingers picking nervously at teeth—which might reveal their real thoughts and opinions. Juror number fifty-six, Nicholas Easter, received more than his share of anxious looks. He worried the jury consultants, as they hadn't been able to find out very much about him.

A lawsuit is brought against Pynex, a tobacco company, by the widow of a man who smoked cigarettes all his life. She feels that Pynex is responsible for her husband's death. The tobacco company—not surprisingly!—disagrees with her, arguing that people are free to make their own life-style choices, including whether to smoke or not. The verdict is of great importance to both sides, but the tobacco company especially cannot afford to lose. If the widow wins her case, it will mean disaster not just for Pynex but for the tobacco industry in general.

The four largest tobacco companies in the country are therefore prepared to pay a lot of money in order to make sure that the jury reach the 'right' verdict. They employ a man, Rankin Fitch, who has a lot of experience in secretly influencing juries—but he is not the only person involved in suspicious activities. One of the jurors is also trying to control what the jury thinks and does—but why is he doing this, and whose side is he on?

John Grisham was born on February 8, 1955, in Jonesboro, Arkansas. His father worked as a builder and a cotton farmer, and his mother was a homemaker. Encouraged by his mother to love books, Grisham soon became an enthusiastic reader, especially of John Steinbeck, who was his favorite writer.

In 1977, Grisham graduated from Mississippi State University with his first degree, and four years later he graduated from law school. He was especially interested in criminal and general law, and he made extensive use of this knowledge in his later career as a novelist. Grisham worked as a small-town general lawyer in Southaven for ten years, and was also elected as a Democrat to the Mississippi House of Representatives in 1983. He was an extremely busy man, working sixty to seventy hours a week in his law practice, but he still found time for his favorite hobby—writing.

In 1984, he began writing his first novel, *A Time to Kill*. He would get up at 5 o'clock in the morning to work on his book before going to his law practice. *A Time to Kill* eventually came out in 1988, but was not a great success. Three years later, however, his second novel, *The Firm*, was published, and that changed his life. It was an immediate success and Paramount Pictures bought the story for $600,000. Suddenly everybody wanted to read John Grisham!

Grisham gave up his law practice and political work, and became a full-time writer. Since 1988, he has written twenty novels and one non-fiction book—most of them best-sellers. In an interview in 2006, Grisham said that he usually took only six months to write a book. *The Runaway Jury*, published in 1996, was his seventh novel. Other legal thrillers include *The Pelican Brief* (1992), *The Client* (1993), *The Chamber* (1994), *The Rainmaker* (1995), and *The Brethren* (2000), all of which are Penguin Readers. In January 2008, Grisham's first fictional legal thriller for three years—*The Appeal*—was published.

Many of Grisham's stories have been made into movies, which has, of course, greatly increased his international popularity. The first movie of one of his stories was *The Firm*, which came to movie theaters in 1993, with Tom Cruise and Gene Hackman in the leading roles. Julia Roberts and Denzel Washington were in *The Pelican Brief* (1993), and the movie of his first novel, *A*

Time to Kill, came out in 1996, starring Sandra Bullock, Samuel L. Jackson, and Kevin Spacey. *Runaway Jury* was released in 2003, with Dustin Hoffman as Wendall Rohr, and Gene Hackman as Rankin Fitch. The most recent movie of a book by Grisham is *Christmas with the Kranks* (2004), based on a non-legal story, *Skipping Christmas* (2001).

John Grisham lives with his family on their two farms in Mississippi and Virginia.

Grisham's books have touched readers everywhere. Almost all his novels are about law, justice, and the court system. They show in great detail the lives of lawyers, judges, and clients. His stories are always very complicated, but they are also entertaining and exciting. In a typical Grisham thriller, honest, ordinary people find themselves in difficulty, even danger, when they fight large, powerful, dishonest organizations. For example, in *A Time to Kill*, his first book, a black man cannot find justice because of the color of his skin; in *The Firm*, a young law school graduate's life is in danger because he discovers the truth about his law firm's criminal activities; in *The Pelican Brief*, a law student fears for her life after she discovers the truth about the deaths of two judges; in *The Rainmaker*, a powerful insurance company tries to refuse a dying boy life-saving treatment; and in this book, *The Runaway Jury*, a widow finds herself in a seemingly impossible legal battle with the four largest tobacco companies in the United States. In all these stories, and many others, if the ordinary people in trouble are not lawyers themselves, there are lawyers who put themselves and their families in danger in order to defend them.

In a world where our lives are increasingly governed by impersonal, powerful forces beyond our control, there are messages of hope for us all in John Grisham stories. Large organizations *can* be defeated if ordinary people are courageous enough. Good humans *can* defeat evil machines.

Chapter 1   The Big Four

High above the water in a modern beach house in Mississippi, four gentlemen enjoyed drinks and waited for a visitor. Normally their work required them to be enemies. This afternoon, however, they'd played golf and eaten grilled seafood together. Each of the men was CEO★ of a large public corporation. These corporations were extremely successful; the smallest had sales of six hundred million dollars, the largest four billion dollars. Although they manufactured other things, their real profits came from cigarettes—the companies represented here were responsible for 98 percent of all cigarettes sold in the United States and Canada.

The tobacco business was becoming more and more unpopular. The Big Four, as the four corporations were known in financial circles, were attacked by the public, the medical profession and even some politicians. And now, the lawyers were pursuing them. The survivors of dead smokers were suing them, claiming that cigarettes caused lung cancer. There had been sixteen trials. Until now, the tobacco companies had managed to win every case, but the pressure was increasing. If they lost a single one, they'd face possible claims from millions of people.

To help fight these court cases, the Big Four had put together a sum of money called The Fund. The Fund was a secret. Officially, it didn't exist. The money in it was used to hire the best defense lawyers for the trials. It paid for well-spoken experts to help persuade people that cigarette smoking didn't necessarily kill you, and the cleverest jury consultants. Before a trial, the jury consultants' job was to find out all they could about possible

★ CEO: Chief Executive Officer

1

jurors, so they could predict whether they might be sympathetic to the tobacco companies' case or not.

The Fund was managed by a man called Rankin Fitch. The four CEOs disliked him, but they listened to what he said and, when necessary, obeyed the instructions he gave. He'd directed eight trials without a loss. Now they were waiting for him to arrive to tell them about the latest trial, *Wood* v. *Pynex*. Pynex was the third largest of the Big Four; its CEO was D. Martin Jankle.

"Fitch is here." The four men each reached for their drinks as Fitch walked into the room. He was a big man in a dark suit; he looked important. An assistant handed him a glass of water, and he waved away a plate of seafood.

"A brief summary, gentlemen. At the moment, the entire defense team is working non-stop, and this will continue through the weekend. Investigations into possible jurors are on schedule. Trial lawyers are ready, witnesses are prepared, all our experts are already in town."

"What about the jurors?" asked Jankle. It was his corporation's lawsuit, and so he was the most nervous. "One problem juror can be poison."

"I'm aware of that," Fitch replied coldly.

"I assume the plaintiff's lawyers are ready?" asked another CEO.

"Safe assumption," said Fitch. This latest challenge to the tobacco companies had been organized carefully. There were eight lawyers at the last count, financed by eight of the largest law firms in the country, who'd each contributed a million dollars. The lawyers had picked the plaintiff, the widow of a man named Jacob L. Wood. They'd picked the place, on the Mississippi coast, because juries in Biloxi could be generous in this kind of case. They were even lucky with the judge, the Honorable★ Frederick

★ Honorable, Your Honor: titles given to a judge.

Harkin. He'd previously been a plaintiff's lawyer. The opposition were certainly ready.

This wasn't an ordinary tobacco case, and everyone in the room knew it.

"How long will the trial last?" Jankle finally asked.

"Four to six weeks. Jury selection goes fast here," replied Fitch.

"How long should we stay in town?"

"I don't care. You can leave now, or you can wait until the jury is picked. You all have big jets. If I need you, I can find you." He was suddenly ready to leave. "Anything else?"

Not a word.

♦

Wendall Rohr, the main lawyer for the plaintiff, had made and lost his first fortune before he was fifty. He made his second fortune and swore never to lose it. His energies were directed at suing American corporations on behalf of injured people. He'd met Celeste Wood, widow of Jacob Wood, through a young lawyer. Jacob Wood had died at the age of fifty-one after smoking three packs of cigarettes a day for almost thirty years.

Rohr had raised the first million dollars to fight the case, and then more money had flowed in. His plan was simple and smart. If he won this case, more people would decide to sue. With a hundred million smokers out there, he'd be busy for the rest of his working life.

Rohr operated from offices near the courthouse, and his team was working hard investigating possible jurors. The tobacco lawyers were down the street working just as hard. Nothing rivaled the thrill of big lawsuits.

♦

By 8 A.M. on Monday, a crowd was gathering outside the Biloxi courthouse. There were Wall Street financial analysts who were specialists in the price of tobacco shares, sent to follow the early developments of the trial. There was a group of people growing larger by the minute, each holding a piece of paper—a jury summons. Seven deputies had been assigned to security duties.

At eight-thirty the doors to the courtroom, on the second floor, opened. A court official, Gloria Lane, checked each summons, greeted the people she knew, and organized them into their seats. There were 194 possible jurors. All were given forms to complete. The lawyers arrived in dark suits, and tried to look at the jurors without being noticed.

Behind the lawyers sat the jury consultants, watching the possible jurors for any gestures—arms folded across the chest, or fingers picking nervously at teeth—which might reveal their real thoughts and opinions. Juror number fifty-six, Nicholas Easter, received more than his share of anxious looks. He worried the jury consultants, as they hadn't been able to find out very much about him.

The last lawyer into the room was Wendall Rohr. He stared at the possible jurors. These were his people. This was his case, in his home town. He nodded at a couple, grinned at another. Together they'd find the truth.

Rankin Fitch was also in court, pretending to read a newspaper.

Then Judge Harkin arrived. He completed a short welcoming speech. The lawsuit had begun four years ago, and the documents now filled eleven boxes. Each side had already spent millions to reach this point.

The jury selection started. Six people over the age of sixty-five who hadn't been identified by the computer were free to leave. Five of them left.

"Is anybody legally blind?" the Judge asked. Slowly a hand was raised from the center of the pack. Juror number sixty-three, Mr. Herman Grimes, age fifty-nine, computer programmer, white, married, no kids. What was this? Did nobody know this man was blind? The jury consultants whispered on both sides.

"Mr. Grimes, you are excused from jury duty. You're free to go."

Herman Grimes didn't move. He just looked at whatever he could see and said, "Why do I have to leave?"

"Because you're blind."

"I know that. Who says blind people can't serve on juries? You tell me why. If it's written in the law, the law is unfair, and I'll sue. If it isn't written in the law, I'll sue even faster."

The law said that a blind person *may* be excused from jury service, so the Judge decided not to insist. "On second thoughts, Mr. Grimes, I think you'd be an excellent juror. Please sit down."

Herman nodded politely. "Thank you, sir."

The Judge continued to release possible jurors with physical problems. At noon, thirteen had been dismissed. By 3 P. M. the number remaining was down to 159. Then the group were asked about any non-medical problems. Eleven more were dismissed, and another form was given out, with instructions to the jurors that they should complete it by nine the next morning.

♦

The form included questions like, *Do you smoke cigarettes? Do you want to stop? Has any member of your family, or anyone you know well, suffered any disease or illness directly linked to smoking cigarettes?* Other questions explored their opinions on tax and smokers' rights. Then: *Do you know any of the lawyers working on the case? Do you know any of the possible witnesses?*

Nicholas Easter made another cup of coffee. He'd spent an hour with the questions last night, and another hour this morning. He knew that handwriting experts would study everything he wrote. He wanted to appear neat, thoughtful, and intelligent, a juror that both sides would love.

5

Many of the questions had been used in the Cimmino tobacco case last year in Allentown, Pennsylvania. Nicholas had been a possible juror in that case too. But then he'd been known as David Lancaster, a part-time film student with a beard and glasses. He hadn't been selected for the jury. A month later, he'd shaved his beard, thrown away his glasses, and left town.

Nicholas knew that there were people on both sides trying to find out about his past. His present apartment was only a temporary home. It was basic, but although he had a better address four blocks away, he couldn't risk being seen there.

♦

In court on the second day, the forms were collected from the possible jurors and six more were excused for personal reasons. Then the show began. Wendall Rohr introduced the plaintiff, Celeste Woods, to the court. A small woman of fifty-five, she tried to look as if she was still saddened over the death of her husband, although he'd been dead for four years. In fact, she'd almost remarried, an event which Rohr had persuaded her to cancel when he heard about it. She could marry after the trial, he told her.

Rohr started questioning the possible jurors about their previous jury service and their opinions on the rights of victims and the price of insurance.

The jury had a lunch break; Gloria Lane and her staff handed out box lunches to the lawyers, containing thin sandwiches and red apples. This was going to be a working lunch for them. Outside the courtroom, forms were being analyzed by the jury consultants and the results were being fed into computers. After three hours' discussion with the lawyers, the Judge removed another thirty-one names. The group was down to 111.

♦

The following morning, it was the turn of the main lawyer for Pynex, Durwood Cable, senior partner for Whitney & Cable & White. His opponent, Wendall Rohr, was friendly and sociable; Cable, on the other hand, seemed quieter. He talked slowly, but his gray eyes missed nothing.

"My name is Durwood Cable and I represent Pynex, a company that has been making cigarettes for ninety years." There, he wasn't ashamed of it! He did an expert job of persuading his audience that his client was almost likeable. Cable then talked about the freedom to choose whether to smoke cigarettes or not. He asked a lot of questions, got a few responses, and finished at noon, in time for a quick lunch.

Before three o'clock, the lawyers on both sides had to agree on the final jury selection. According to the rules, each side could ask for a number of strikes, which meant that a possible juror could be dismissed for no reason. Because of the importance of this case, Judge Harkin had granted each side the right to do this ten times, instead of the usual four. The process started. Out of the first thirty names, ten were selected. Finally, the jury was complete, and Nicholas Easter had become the eleventh juror for *Wood* v. *Pynex*.

When the courtroom was opened at three, Judge Harkin called out the names of the chosen twelve. Nicholas, twenty-seven, was the second youngest juror. There were nine whites, three blacks, seven women, five men—one blind. In the corner of the jury box, there were three extra jurors. These would replace any member of the jury who had to leave the jury for some reason.

The Judge forbade the jurors from discussing the case with anyone, and with a pleasant smile, dismissed them for the night.

Chapter 2 The Case Opens

At eight-thirty in the morning, Nicholas slipped through the unlocked back door of the courthouse and went up to the second floor. He knew the building well. Three weeks earlier, unnoticed, when there was no one around, he'd explored the area around the courtroom, including the Judge's chambers, the witness rooms and, of course, the jury room. He went there now, and found Lou Dell sitting outside the room, reading a romantic novel.

"Good morning. Can I help you?" Her entire face was one large smile.

"Nicholas Easter," he said as he reached for her outstretched hand. She found his name on her paperwork.

"Welcome to the jury room. Is this your first trial?"

"Yes."

"Come on," she said, pulling him into the room. "Coffee and cakes are over here. I made these cookies myself."

Nicholas poured black coffee into a plastic cup. There was a list of instructions for the jurors from Judge Harkin, including the order that they couldn't discuss the case with anyone. They couldn't even discuss the case with each other, until instructed by the Judge. Nicholas signed the list at the bottom, as requested.

The door opened with a kick, and Mr. Herman Grimes entered with his walking stick tapping along in front of him. His wife was close behind, describing the room to him under her breath. Nicholas introduced himself.

"My favorite uncle's blind," Nicholas said. "I'd consider it an honor if you'd allow me to assist you during the trial."

"Thank you," said Herman, after a brief pause.

"Thank you, sir," his wife said.

♦

At ten o'clock, Judge Harkin looked around the crowded courtroom and decided that everyone was in place. "Bring in the jury," he said. The jurors walked in.

"Good morning," said the Judge. "Do we have a foreman?"

"It's me, Your Honor," Herman Grimes said.

The lawyers and jury consultants for the defense were worried by this choice of foreman, but their expressions remained warm and positive.

Nicholas Easter looked cautiously around the courtroom. On the second row, behind the defense, Rankin Fitch sat trying to look uninterested in the jury, but Nicholas knew better. Fitch missed nothing. Fourteen months earlier, Nicholas had seen him in the Cimmino courtroom in Allentown, Pennsylvania. Nicholas knew that Fitch would have investigated his background and found that some of what he'd said wasn't true.

There were also small groups of people whom Nicholas was certain were the jury consultants. The selecting was done, so now they moved to the next phase—watching. They listened to every word spoken by every witness, and predicted how the jury would react. If a witness seemed to make a bad impression on the jury, they could be removed, sent home, and replaced by another witness.

After a sign from the Judge, Wendall Rohr started his opening statement. He told the jury that he'd prove that Mr. Jacob Wood, a fine fellow, developed lung cancer after smoking cigarettes for almost thirty years. The cigarettes killed him. How could they prove that cigarettes caused lung cancer? They'd bring along cancer experts, and talk to people who used to work in the tobacco industry.

Rohr finished in fifty minutes, smiled, and sat down. Durwood Cable, for the defense, spoke for under thirty minutes. He calmly assured the jurors that Pynex had its own experts who would clearly explain that cigarettes don't cause lung cancer. Cable spoke without notes, looking carefully into the eyes of each juror. His voice and stare were honest. You wanted to believe this man.

♦

The first crisis occurred at lunch. Judge Harkin announced the noon break at 12:10, and the jurors left the court. Lou Dell took them to the jury room.

"Just have a seat," she said, "and lunch will be here in a moment."

Herman Grimes took a seat at the head of the table next to Millie Dupree, a kind woman of fifty who actually knew another blind person. Nicholas introduced himself to Lonnie Shaver, the only black man on the jury and the manager of a grocery store.

Twenty minutes passed, and no lunch appeared. At twelve-thirty, Nicholas said, "Hey, Herman, where's our lunch?"

"I'm just the foreman," Herman answered with a smile, as the room was suddenly quiet.

Nicholas walked to the door and asked Lou Dell to come in. "We're hungry," he said.

Lou Dell looked at the other eleven faces and said, "It's on the way."

"Where's it coming from?" he demanded.

"O'Reilly's restaurant. Just around the corner."

"Listen," said Nicholas. "We can't go out and eat a nice lunch like normal people. So if lunch is going to be here, I hope there isn't going to be a problem every day. I suggest you get on the phone and find out where it is, or I'll discuss it with Judge Harkin."

The door closed.

"That was a bit hard, don't you think?" asked Millie Dupree.

"Maybe, and if it was, I'll apologize," said Nicholas. "But if we don't get things organized at the beginning, they'll forget about us. Do you realize that in almost every trial, they allow the jurors to go out and eat?"

"How do you know?" asked Millie Dupree.

"I know a little about the system. I had two years of law school." The other jurors were impressed.

No food had arrived by 12:45.

"It should be here soon," said Lou Dell nervously. "I'm really sorry."

"Where's the men's room?" asked Nicholas.

Lou Dell gave him directions, but Nicholas walked past the door and out of the courthouse to Mary Mahoney's, a local restaurant. Nicholas had done the same walk a week ago—and had even eaten at a table close to Judge Harkin's. He went up to the Judge's table.

"Sorry to interrupt, sir," Nicholas said.

"What are you doing here?" Harkin asked.

"I'm here on behalf of your jury. While you're having a nice lunch here, we're sitting in a tiny room waiting for food. We're hungry, and we're upset."

Harkin stood up. "Well, let's go and see."

When they got back to the jury room, the table was bare. No food. The time was 1:05.

Lou Dell suddenly arrived. She was breathless. "I've just talked to O'Reilly's," she said. "Someone called them to say we wouldn't need lunch until one-thirty."

"These people are starving," said the Judge. He turned to the jury. "I'm very sorry. This won't happen again." He paused, looked at his watch, and smiled. "I'm inviting you to follow me to Mary Mahoney's and join me for lunch."

The restaurant served the jurors with delicious grilled seafood. Nicholas was the hero of the day.

Later, Mr. O'Reilly met with Judge Harkin. He swore on a Bible that he'd talked to a woman who said she was ringing from the courthouse. She'd instructed him to deliver lunch at exactly one-thirty.

◆

The trial's first witness was the dead man, Jacob Wood, testifying on a video which had been filmed a few months before his death. He was thin and pale, and sounded sick. He was fifty-one and looked twenty years older.

When the jury felt sleepy, the Judge gave them a break. The four smokers needed a cigarette, and Lou Dell took them to a separate room.

"If you can't stop smoking after this trial, something's wrong," she said, jokingly.

The four didn't smile. Jerry Fernandez, thirty-eight, a car salesman with casino debts and a bad marriage, lit his cigarette first. Then he passed his lighter to the three women.

"Here's to Jacob Wood," Jerry said. The three women said nothing—they were busy smoking. One of them was a tall woman with a long pointed nose, called Sylvia Taylor-Tatum. "I wonder who's next?" Jerry continued.

"I guess all those doctors," Sylvia replied, sucking hard on her cigarette.

◆

The woman's name was Marlee; at least that was the name she'd chosen for this period of her life. She was thirty, with short brown hair and brown eyes. She'd been in the courtroom before and she knew her way around. She sat in the back row, and just before the Judge arrived she asked one of the deputies to deliver a letter to Rankin Fitch.

Fitch was surprised to see his name on the envelope. No one knew his name, except his employees and clients. He read the note:

Dear Mr. Fitch:
Tomorrow, juror number two, Easter, will wear a gray and red sweater, white socks, and brown leather shoes.

Fitch went up to the deputy who was standing by the courtroom door. "Who gave you this?"

"A woman. I don't know her name." Fitch questioned the deputy about her appearance and voice. With José, his driver, he looked around the first floor of the courthouse. Then, as if they were just enjoying some fresh air, the two men walked around the outside of the courthouse. Who was she, and what was going on?

♦

Fitch had thought about entering Easter's apartment before, but now he knew it was necessary. He sent José and another man, Doyle, to the apartment building while Easter was in court. Inside, Doyle photographed the apartment. He was there for no more than ten minutes.

Nicholas left the courthouse on foot and stopped at O'Reilly's for some food. He was certain he was being followed. When he got to his apartment, he entered a four-number code on the door before he unlocked it. He went to his computer and found that an illegal entry had occurred at 4:52 P.M. The secret camera, hidden above the refrigerator, had filmed Doyle. Nicholas watched the video and stared at Doyle's face. He'd never seen him before. Nicholas smiled as he saw Doyle looking at his computer. It was impossible to enter. Doyle couldn't even find the power switch.

♦

At eight the next morning, Fitch was hiding in a van by Easter's apartment and watched him walk out into the sunshine. Fitch looked out of the van window. "I don't believe it!" Gray and red sweater, white socks, brown shoes. Fitch went straight to his office. "We have to find the girl," he said. "She has something for us."

His office was in the back of an empty store. No one noticed the place and it was just a short walk from the courthouse. Two men with guns guarded the door at all times. The furniture was cheap, but the office was full of the latest technology. The walls of one room were covered with photos of the jurors.

The room at the back was the smallest, and was kept locked. It was a viewing room. One of Fitch's people had hidden a tiny camera in a document case which was placed in the courtroom under the defense table and which secretly filmed all the jurors. In the viewing room, two jury consultants watched the results on a large screen. When Fitch talked to Cable, he could tell him how the jurors seemed to be feeling. Cable, however, didn't know about the hidden camera.

♦

The deal was organized over a three-hour lunch. Luther Vandemeer, CEO of Trellco, one of the Big Four tobacco companies, and his friend, Larry Zell, of Listing Foods, had already talked about it on the phone. Trellco wasn't in court this time, but the Big Four had to stand together. Zell understood. He'd worked for Trellco for seventeen years.

There was a small, regional grocery company, Hadley Brothers, which owned stores along the Mississippi coast. One store was in Biloxi and its manager was a smart young black man called Lonnie Shaver, who by chance was on the jury in the Pynex trial. Vandemeer wanted one of Listing Food's divisions, SuperHouse, a much larger group of grocery stores, to purchase Hadley Brothers. It would be a small deal, and nothing could go wrong. Listing and Trellco were totally independent of each other, and Listing was already in the grocery store business. Later, of course, there would need to be a reorganization of the company, and pressure could be put on Lonnie Shaver to support the defense.

They needed to act quickly. The trial was only due to last for four more weeks.

Chapter 3   Lonnie Shaver's Opportunity

Easter made sure he was easy to follow over the weekend. On Saturday he worked all day selling computers, then he returned to his apartment and didn't leave it.

On Sunday he drove to the harbor, where he met Jerry Fernandez. They left in a fishing boat with two others, and returned eight and a half hours later with red faces, a can full of fish, and a boat full of empty beer cans. Fishing was the first hobby of Nicholas Easter that anyone had been able to discover. And Jerry was the first friend.

There was no sign of the girl.

♦

She waited only until Monday morning, thirty minutes before the trial restarted. Fitch was in his office. An assistant, Konrad, said, "There's a phone call you might like to take."

"Her name?"

"She won't say."

"Any idea how she got the number?"

"No."

"Are you tracing it?"

"Yes. Give us a minute. Keep her on the line."

Fitch lifted the telephone receiver. "Yes," he said, as nicely as possible.

"Is this Mr. Fitch?" she asked, quite pleasantly.

"It is. And who is this?"

"Marlee. In about twenty minutes, juror number twelve,

Fernandez, will walk into the courtroom holding a copy of *Sports Illustrated*, the October 12 issue."

"I see," said Fitch. "Anything else?"

"No, not now."

Konrad raced in. "The call came from a pay phone in Gulfpoint, a convenience store."

"What a surprise," said Fitch as he grabbed his jacket and began straightening his tie. "I guess I'll run to court."

◆

In the jury room Nicholas waited until the general conversation died down. He said loudly, "Well, did anyone get bribed or followed over the weekend?" There were a few laughs, but no confessions.

"Why does the Judge keep asking questions like that?" asked Millie Dupree.

"In similar cases there have been some problems with the jurors," Nicholas explained.

"I don't think we should discuss this," Herman said.

"Why not? It's harmless. This isn't about evidence. This is about . . . " He hesitated a second for effect, then continued, "This is about trying to control the jury." Nicholas had the jurors' attention. "There was a tobacco trial, very similar to this, in Quitman County, Mississippi, about seven years ago. There was some pretty shocking behavior, before and during the trial. Judge Harkin is watching us carefully. Lots of people are watching us."

"Who?" asked Millie.

"Both sides," answered Nicholas. "Both sides hire these jury consultants and they come here to help pick the perfect jury. The perfect jury is one that will deliver the verdict that they want. They study us before we're selected."

"How do they do that?" one of the jurors asked.

"Well, they photograph us, our apartments, our offices, and

our kids. It's just legal, but it's close to being illegal. They might check our tax records and talk to our neighbors."

All eleven jurors were listening, trying to remember if they'd seen any strangers hiding around street corners with cameras. Nicholas drank some coffee and continued: "After the jury's been picked, it's a little different. Now they're only watching fifteen people—the twelve jurors and the three extra jurors. Throughout the trial, each side will have jury consultants in the courtroom trying to read our reactions. They usually sit on the first two rows. They're well dressed and they stare at us all the time."

"I thought those folks were newspaper reporters," said another juror, retired Colonel Frank Herrera.

"I hadn't noticed," said Herman Grimes. Everyone smiled.

"Watch them today," Nicholas said. "In fact, I have a great idea. There's one woman who I'm almost positive is a jury consultant for the defense. Every morning since the trial began, she's been on the front row behind Durwood Cable. When we go out this morning, let's stare at her. All twelve of us."

"Even me?" Herman asked.

"Yes, Herm, even you. Just turn to ten o'clock, and stare with the rest of us."

"Why are we playing games?" asked Sylvia Taylor-Tatum.

"Why not? What else have we got to do for the next eight hours? Let's do it while Judge Harkin is reminding us about all the rules. That always takes ten minutes."

♦

Lou Dell came for them at nine. Nicholas held two magazines— one of which was *Sports Illustrated*. He walked beside Jerry Fernandez until they came to the courtroom, then said to his new friend, "Want something to read?"

Jerry took the magazine, "Sure, thanks," he said. They walked through the door into the courtroom.

17

Fitch knew Fernandez, juror number twelve, would have the magazine, but the sight of it was still a shock. His surprise quickly turned to excitement. Marlee was clearly working on the outside; maybe there were two or three or four members of the jury who were plotting with her. It didn't matter how many jurors were involved; Fitch just wanted to make a deal.

The jury consultant's name was Ginger. She'd sat through dozens of trials. She looked at the jury and waited for the Judge to greet them, which he did. Most of the jurors nodded and smiled at the Judge. Then all of them, including the blind man, turned and stared directly at her.

She looked away.

Judge Harkin continued asking the jurors one question after another and he, too, quickly noticed that the jury were looking at the same person.

They kept staring, all together. Nicholas found it difficult not to laugh. His luck was unbelievable. Two rows behind Ginger sat Rankin Fitch. It was difficult to tell exactly who the jurors were staring at—Ginger or Fitch. Ginger certainly thought it was her. She found some notes to read. Fitch felt helpless as the twelve faces studied him.

Judge Harkin finished his questions quickly. "Thank you, ladies and gentlemen. Now we will continue with Dr. Milton Fricke."

After Dr. Fricke had spoken, there was a short break as a new witness, Dr. Robert Bronsky, was called by Wendall Rohr. Fitch was in his office when the call came.

"It's Marlee, line four," Konrad whispered.

"Trace the call," Fitch ordered. "Hello."

"Mr. Fitch?" came the familiar voice.

"Yes."

"Do you know why they were staring at you?"

"No."

"I'll tell you tomorrow. And if you keep tracing the calls, I'll stop calling."

Konrad arrived with the expected news that the call had been made from a payphone.

♦

On Tuesday morning, Nicholas arrived at the jury room early. There were new cups and saucers. Nicholas claimed to hate coffee from a plastic cup, and two of the other jurors said they felt the same. The Judge had agreed to his request.

Retired Colonel Frank Herrera arrived just after eight.

"Morning, Colonel," Nicholas said warmly. "You're early."

"So are you."

"I know. I couldn't sleep. I was dreaming of black lungs."

Herrera sat down across the table. "I smoked for ten years in the Army," he said. "But I had the good sense to stop."

"Some people can't, I guess. Like Jacob Wood." The Colonel made a sound of disgust. "Why did you stop?"

"Because cigarettes are poison. Everybody knows that."

If Herrera had given those opinions on the pre-trial forms, he wouldn't have been selected. But he probably wanted to be on the jury. He was retired, bored with golf, and tired of his wife.

"So should cigarettes be illegal?" Nicholas asked.

"No, I think people shouldn't be stupid and smoke three packs a day for almost thirty years. What do they expect?" There was no doubt that his mind was made up.

"You should have said this during jury selection. We were asked questions just like these," said Nicholas.

Herrera's cheeks went red, but he hesitated for a second. This guy Easter knew the law. "Yes, well, I can be persuaded, you know," Herrera said.

♦

19

After a day in court looking at diagrams of lungs and listening to medical explanations from Dr. Bronsky, Lonnie drove to his supermarket.

"We have guests from Head Office for you," an assistant manager said with a frown.

In his office Lonnie found three men.

"Lonnie, good to see you," said Troy Hadley, son of one of the owners. He quickly introduced the others. "Listen, Lonnie, Ken and Ben here are from a company called SuperHouse, and, well, for lots of reasons, my dad and my uncle have decided to sell all seventeen stores to them."

Lonnie was finding it hard to swallow. "Why?"

"Two main reasons. Number one, my dad is sixty-eight, and Al, my uncle, has just had surgery, as you know. Also, SuperHouse is offering a good price. It's time to sell."

"Will this store be closed?" Lonnie asked, almost in defeat.

Ken picked up a piece of paper. "Well, there are always changes when this sort of thing happens. But we see a future for you with us, Lonnie. We're ashamed to admit that we don't have an African-American in a management position. We want this to change. We'd like you to come to Charlotte as soon as possible and spend a few days with us. When can you come?"

In a minute Lonnie had gone from near-unemployment to promotion in a new company. He said with obvious disappointment, "I'm on jury service. But what about the weekends?"

"Can you do this weekend?"

"Sure," said Lonnie.

♦

The first person Nicholas saw the following morning in court was the man who'd broken into his apartment. Nicholas had already decided what to do. He wrote a note and asked for it to be handed to the Judge.

Judge:
That man out there, left side, third row from the front, white shirt, blue and green tie, was following me yesterday. It's the second time I've seen him. Can we find out who he is?
Nicholas Easter

The Judge called a ten-minute break, and asked for Nicholas. "Now, where did you see this man?"

Nicholas didn't mention the video, but told the Judge that he'd seen the man a couple of times recently.

The Judge relaxed slightly. "Mr. Easter, have any of the other jurors mentioned anything like this?"

"No, sir."

"Will you tell me if they do? If there's something wrong I need to know. You can send a note through Lou Dell."

"Well, there is something perhaps you ought to know . . . " He hesitated. "Colonel Herrera thinks that anyone who smokes three packs of cigarettes a day for almost thirty years deserves what he gets."

The Judge digested this information. "Mr. Easter, I'm not asking you to spy on the other jurors. But I am worried about this jury because of the pressure from the outside. If you see or hear anything, please tell me."

"Sure, Judge."

Chapter 4   More Telephone Calls

The defense's questioning of Bronsky ended late Thursday afternoon, and Marlee struck on Friday morning. Konrad took the first call at 7:25.

21

"Good morning, Fitch," she said sweetly, when she was put through.

"Good morning, Marlee," Fitch answered with a happy voice, his best effort at pleasantness. "And how are you?"

"Fabulous. Juror number two, Easter, will wear a light blue shirt, faded jeans, and running shoes. And he'll bring with him a copy of *Rolling Stone*, October issue. Got that?"

"Yes. When can we get together and talk?"

"When I'm ready."

Pang, one of Fitch's technicians, was sitting in a coffee shop near Easter's apartment. On time, Easter left his apartment and started his walk to the courthouse. Of course, he was wearing exactly what she'd promised.

Marlee's second call came from a different number.

"Something new for you, Fitch. You'll love it. Guess what the jurors are going to do today."

"Tell me."

"They're going to do the Pledge of Allegiance."★

Marlee's third call went to the offices of Wendall Rohr. She was going to send a fax which must be handed to Mr. Rohr before he left for court. The fax stated which clothes Nicholas Easter would wear that day, and hinted at the Pledge. Rohr called an emergency meeting.

◆

Before the court started, Nicholas waited for a pause in the conversation. "Hey, Herman, I have an idea."

By now, Herman knew the other eleven voices from memory. "Yes, Nicholas," he said.

Nicholas raised his voice so everyone could hear him. "Well,

★ Pledge of Allegiance: a statement by American citizens of their loyalty to the United States.

when I was a kid, we started each day at school with the Pledge of Allegiance. Every time I see a flag early in the morning, I have this desire to give the Pledge. And in the courtroom, we have this beautiful flag behind the Judge."

"You want to do the Pledge of Allegiance out there in open court?" asked Colonel Herrera.

"Can't see anything wrong with that," said Jerry Fernandez, who'd earlier agreed to support Nicholas.

"You're not playing games, are you?" asked the Colonel.

Nicholas looked at him with aching eyes and said, "My father was killed in Vietnam. That flag means a lot to me."

The plan was agreed. The jurors entered the courtroom. Just before Judge Harkin started his standard speech reminding them that they mustn't have unauthorized contact with anyone, he realized that the jurors were still standing. With their hands on their hearts, and led by Nicholas, they said the Pledge of Allegiance.

Judge Harkin's initial reaction was of disbelief. He glanced at Rohr and Cable, who were open mouthed. Then he stood. Halfway through the Pledge he joined in. Suddenly it seemed important that everyone joined in. The lawyers certainly couldn't show any disloyalty.

From the back row, Fitch watched in amazement. A jury taking control of a courtroom! It was extraordinary that Marlee knew it was going to happen. It was exciting that she was playing games with him. But Fitch at least had some idea of what was happening. Wendall Rohr, on the other hand, felt completely defeated. He was shocked by the sight of Easter dressed exactly as the fax had said, and then starting the Pledge. He stared at the jury, especially Easter, and wondered what was going on.

The Pledge finished and the jurors sat down. Judge Harkin seemed determined to act as if this was normal behavior.

"I believe we're ready for a new witness," he said.

Rohr stood, still shocked, and said, "The plaintiff calls Dr. Hilo Kilvan."

The next expert witness entered the courtroom.

♦

Lonnie was collected early Saturday morning by a company jet, and was flown to Charlotte. Ken met him at the airport in a company van, and fifteen minutes later they arrived at the SuperHouse headquarters. Ken and Ben showed him around. They had coffee with George Teaker, the CEO, in his large office, and then Lonnie was shown a video about the company. According to the video, SuperHouse was going to grow by 15 percent a year for the next six years. Profits would be amazing.

When the video finished, a young man arrived with details about health care, share options, and vacations. After lunch in a smart restaurant, there were more meetings and another video. By now, Lonnie needed some fresh air, and Ken suggested that they could go and play golf. Lonnie had never played golf before, a fact that Ken knew, but he suggested that they go and get some sunshine anyway. They drove through neat farms and tree-lined roads until they reached the country club.

Lonnie was nervous about entering a smart country club and decided to leave if he saw no other black faces. But George Teaker was in the club lounge with two black gentlemen. They all greeted Lonnie warmly and he felt much better. They drank and talked and planned the future. Lonnie stayed the night in the country club, and woke the next morning with a slight headache.

That morning there were two brief meetings. The first was with George Teaker, who wanted Lonnie to run the Biloxi store for ninety days, under a new contract. If all went well, he'd be transferred to a larger store. They were then joined by a lawyer, Taunton, who handed Lonnie a proposed contract of employment.

"Look over it," Taunton said, tapping his chin with a designer pen, "and we'll talk next week." He took out a notepad. "Just a few questions," he said. The questions were routine. Then he asked, "Have you, in your capacity as store manager, been involved in litigation?"

"Yes, I have," replied Lonnie. "About four years ago, an old man slipped and fell on a wet floor. He sued. "

"Did it go to trial?" asked Taunton. He knew every detail.

"No," replied Lonnie. "The claim was settled out of court."

Taunton glanced at Teaker and said, "This tobacco trial in Biloxi could be serious for companies like ours. If the plaintiff wins the case and there's a big verdict, there will be a lot more tobacco litigation. The lawyers will go crazy. They'll bankrupt the tobacco companies."

"We make a lot of money from tobacco sales, Lonnie," Teaker said, with perfect timing.

"There has to be an end to these trials. The tobacco industry has never lost one of them. I think their record is something like fifty-five wins." He took a deep breath. "Sorry if I said too much. But this trial is so important."

Lonnie thought about this. Taunton was a lawyer, so he wouldn't talk about the trial in a way that wasn't appropriate. "No problem," he said.

Taunton was suddenly all smiles and promised to call Lonnie. The meeting was over.

♦

On Monday morning, the jurors met over coffee, and talked about their weekends. Herman was late so he couldn't stop them whispering about the trial.

"I think I was followed at the weekend," said Nicholas

"Why would they follow you?" someone asked.

"That's what the tobacco companies do. They spend millions of dollars selecting us, and more watching us."

"How do you know it's the tobacco company?" asked Sylvia, lighting another cigarette.

"I don't. But they have more money than the plaintiff. In fact they have unlimited funds to fight these cases."

◆

For Wendall Rohr and the plaintiff's team, the weekend had brought no rest. They'd traced Marlee's fax back to a truck stop near Hattiesburg, and obtained an unclear description of a young woman, late twenties, maybe early thirties, wearing a fishing cap, with a face half-hidden by dark glasses. It was the opinion of the eight principal plaintiff's lawyers that this was something new. No one could recall a trial in which a person outside had contacted the lawyers with hints of what the jury might do. They all agreed that she'd be back and that she'd probably ask for money. A deal—money for a verdict.

They didn't dare, however, to plan how they might deal with her. Maybe later, but not now.

Fitch, on the other hand, thought of little else. He'd spent the weekend watching jurors and meeting with lawyers. He'd been pleased with the Ken and Ben show in Charlotte, and had been assured by George Teaker that they could trust Lonnie Shaver. Fitch slept four hours Saturday and five Sunday. He dreamed of the girl Marlee, and what she might bring him. This could be his easiest verdict yet.

◆

Fitch watched the courtroom on Monday from the viewing room in his office. He listened as Dr. Hilo Kilvan continued with his testimony. Fitch's consultants were certain that the plaintiff's witnesses hadn't really made a strong impression on the jurors.

In court, Nicholas sent a note to the Judge saying that he

26

needed to see him urgently. At lunchtime, he went to the Judge's chambers.

"I need to be quick," said Nicholas. "It's Frank Herrera. We talked about him last time. Well, his mind is made up, and I'm afraid he's trying to influence people."

"Is he discussing the case?"

"Once, with me. Herman is very proud of being foreman of the jury, and he won't allow talk about the trial. And another thing." Nicholas opened his case and pulled out a videocassette. He looked at a videocassette recorder in the corner. "May I?"

The Judge nodded. On the video, they watched a man enter Nicholas's apartment. They saw the man, Doyle, taking pictures of the apartment and then leaving. "I was robbed and beaten about five years ago and I almost died. I'm careful about security now," said Nicholas.

◆

Fitch's sandwich was interrupted with the words he was waiting to hear: "The girl's on the line." He grabbed the phone.

"Fitch, baby. It's me, Marlee. Don't know the guy's name, but he's the goon you sent into Easter's apartment on Thursday, just after I gave you the note. Anyway, later, you sent the same goon into the courtroom. That was stupid because Easter recognized him, and he sent a note to the Judge. Are you listening, Fitch?"

Listening, but not breathing. "Yes."

"Well, now the Judge knows that the guy broke into Easter's apartment. So get him out of town, fast."

Two hours later, Doyle was flying to Chicago.

◆

At three-thirty, the jurors were sent back to their room, and Judge Harkin questioned the lawyers about the break-in at Nicholas's apartment. Nicholas was called to the meeting, and the

27

Judge questioned him about the man who'd been following him. Nicholas answered in perfect detail, giving dates and places and also describing the security measures in his apartment. He played the videocassette again. After he'd gone, Judge Harkin and the lawyers considered their options.

Back in court, Judge Harkin apologized for his decision. It was very rare to sequester a jury. But he had no choice in this case. The jurors should leave, go home, pack, and report to the court the next day, ready to spend the next two weeks sequestered.

Chapter 5   The Siesta Motel

On Monday night, Nicholas invited Jerry to go to a casino to celebrate their last hours of freedom. Jerry invited Sylvia Taylor-Tatum. They were becoming friendly—Sylvia was divorced for the second time, and Jerry would soon be divorced for the first.

Lonnie Shaver spent Monday night working. He contacted George Teaker at his home and explained that the jury was going to be sequestered and that the Judge had forbidden any direct phone calls to and from the motel. Teaker was sympathetic, and worried about the result of the trial.

"Our people in New York think a guilty verdict could really damage the economy, especially in our business."

"I'll do what I can," Lonnie promised.

"You've got to help us, Lonnie. I know it's difficult, but you're there, know what I mean?"

"Sure, I understand. I'll do what I can."

♦

Durwood Cable waited until almost nine on Monday evening to talk to Fitch.

"We were embarrassed in court this afternoon," Cable said. "Who was the guy in the apartment?"

"He wasn't one of my men. We have reason to believe that he was a goon employed by Rohr and his boys."

"Can you prove it?"

"I don't have to prove a damn thing. And I don't have to answer any more questions. Your job is to win in court."

"I rarely lose."

Fitch went to the door. "I know. And you're doing a fine job, Cable. You just need a little help from the outside."

♦

Nicholas arrived first with two gym bags filled with clothes. Lou Dell and Willis, a deputy, were waiting outside the jury room to collect the bags and store them. It was 8:20, Tuesday morning.

"How do the bags get from here to the hotel?"

"We'll take them over later," Willis said, "but we have to inspect them first."

"No one is inspecting these bags."

"Judge's orders," said Lou Dell.

"I don't care what the Judge has ordered. No one is inspecting my bags." Nicholas placed them in a corner and walked to the coffeepot.

By 8:45, all twelve jurors were present and the room was full of baggage that Nicholas had rescued and stored. He'd done a fine job of making the jury feel really angry about the question of their baggage. At nine, Lou Dell knocked on the door.

"It's time to go. The Judge is ready for you."

"Tell the Judge we're not coming out," said Nicholas.

The courtroom was full on Tuesday morning, so many people

29

witnessed Lou Dell whispering to the Judge. He wondered what to do. His jury was on strike!

The Judge addressed the court. "Gentlemen, there is a small problem with the jury. I need to speak to them."

When the Judge knocked on the jury door, Nicholas opened it.

"What's the problem?" asked the Judge.

"We don't think it fair that the deputies search our bags."

"Why not? It's routine in all sequestration cases."

"These are our personal possessions. We're not terrorists or drug smugglers. We're not coming out until you promise our bags will be left alone."

"Fine," replied the Judge. "The bags will not be searched. But if I find out that a juror possesses any item which is on the list I gave you yesterday, then that juror could be sent to jail. Do you understand?"

Easter looked round the room at the other jurors. "That's fine, Judge," he said. "But there's one other problem. According to your rules here, we're allowed one personal visit per week. We think we should get more."

The Judge didn't want to have a discussion about it. "Can we agree on two? It's only a couple of weeks," he asked.

"Two, with a possible third," said Nicholas.

"That's fine. Does that suit everybody?"

"Thank you, Your Honor," Herman said loudly.

The jury were ready to enter the courtroom.

News of the break-in to Nicholas's apartment affected the Pynex share price. On the Tuesday morning it started to fall. Then rumors started that the jury had refused to leave the jury room because the testimony offered by the plaintiff was so boring. The share price rose again.

◆

The woman juror that Fitch wanted to influence most was Rikki Coleman. She was a pretty thirty-year-old mother of two. She worked as an administrator in a local hospital, and her husband was a private pilot. Neither of the Colemans smoked and there was no evidence that they drank. Because of her lifestyle, and her job in a hospital, Fitch was afraid of Rikki Coleman as a juror.

Fitch had managed to get hold of medical records for seven out of the twelve jurors, including those of Rikki Coleman. After some investigation, he discovered that while Rikki had been at a small Bible college in Montgomery, Alabama, she'd become pregnant, but had decided not to have the baby. The operation was carried out in a small private women's hospital, a week after her twentieth birthday. The father wasn't named.

Rikki had met her husband a year after she finished college. Fitch was willing to bet a lot of money that he didn't know about Rikki's pregnancy.

◆

The motel was called the Siesta Motel and it was fifty kilometers along the Coast. The trip was made by bus. The jurors felt tired and lonely. Only Nicholas was delighted with sequestration, but he managed to look depressed. The bus was followed by Fitch's boys and two detectives working for Rohr. No one expected the motel address to remain a secret.

The jurors were on the first floor of one wing of the motel. Lou Dell and Willis had rooms by the door leading to the main building. Another deputy, Chuck, had a room at the other end of the hallway. The rooms had been assigned by Judge Harkin himself. The motel TVs only showed hotel movies—no news or other programs—during sequestration. The telephones had been removed. A room at the end of the hall had been made into a sitting room for the jurors; it was quickly given the name of the Party Room. No one could leave the wing without authorization.

The following morning over breakfast, the complaints started.

"I don't understand why we can't have telephones," Nicholas said.

"Why can't we have a cold beer?" asked Jerry. "I have a cold beer every night when I'm at home, maybe two."

The complaining increased until the jurors were ready to rebel.

"We'd better get things sorted out now," said Nicholas seriously. "We're going be here for two weeks, maybe three. I say we talk to Judge Harkin."

Judge Harkin was in his chambers with the lawyers when Gloria Lane entered.

"We have another problem with the jury. They're at the motel and they're not coming until they can talk to you."

The Judge gave a false smile. "Let's go and see them."

♦

Konrad took the first call at 8:02. She didn't want to talk to Fitch; she just wanted to leave a message that the jury were upset and not leaving the motel until the Judge had seen them. At 8:09, she called again and gave Konrad the information that Easter would be wearing a dark shirt over a brown T-shirt, and red socks. At 8:12 she called again and asked to speak to Fitch.

"Good morning, Fitch," she said.

"Good morning, Marlee."

"Do you know the St. Regis Hotel in New Orleans?"

"No."

"It's on Canal Street. There's an open-air bar on the roof. Meet me there at seven tonight."

"Fine."

"And come alone. I'll watch you enter the hotel, and if you bring friends, the meeting's off. And if you attempt to trail me, I'll disappear."

♦

Judge Harkin, Cable, and Rohr were met at the front desk of the motel by Lou Dell, who was scared. She led them to the Party Room.

After a few uncertain hellos, the Judge said, "I'm a little disturbed by this."

Nicholas Easter replied, "We're not in the mood to take any criticism." He'd written down a list of their complaints. The Judge had to agree. Beer would be no problem. Newspapers would be allowed after they'd been checked. Phone calls were possible. Television was allowed, if they promised not to watch the local news. The Judge asked for a no-strike guarantee in the future, but Easter wouldn't promise anything.

On the news of a second strike, Pynex shares moved down two points, but later recovered.

♦

The St. Regis Hotel was watched by Fitch's people from the afternoon, but there was no sign of the girl. Just before seven, Fitch went up in the elevator to the roof and sat down. Several of his people were there, at different tables.

At seven-thirty she appeared from nowhere. She was very pretty, and Fitch guessed her age to be between twenty-eight and thirty-two. The waiter asked if she wanted something to drink. He'd been bribed to remove anything she touched with her fingers—glasses, plates, anything. He wouldn't get the chance.

"Are you hungry?" Fitch asked.

"No. I'm in a hurry. If I stay, your goons can take more photos."

"So why are we here?"

"One meeting leads to another."

"And where do all the meetings lead us?"

"To a verdict."

"For a fee, I'm sure."

"Let's not talk about money now, OK?"

They talked briefly about some of the jurors. Fitch found out little about Marlee's real identity or her relationship with Nicholas Easter. As soon as Marlee had left, Fitch ordered his people to go after her. When she was nearly back home in Biloxi, Marlee told the police that she was being followed. Two of Fitch's goons were arrested.

Later that evening, Nicholas slipped out of the motel and met Marlee, who told him all about her trip to New Orleans.

◆

Wendall Rohr thought the court was tired of listening to scientists talk about lung cancer and smoking. So on Thursday morning he called Lawrence Krigler as his next witness. Lawrence Krigler had worked for Pynex. He'd left in the middle of a lawsuit with the company—he'd sued Pynex and they'd sued him—which had been settled out of court. While he was there, he did research on the possibility of growing an experimental tobacco leaf which contained much less nicotine. But the company wasn't interested. Nicotine was addictive. More nicotine meant more smokers, which meant more sales and more profits.

It was an important moment in the trial. Everyone was listening carefully. Over lunch the jury were silent. Did they really hear right? Did tobacco companies keep nicotine levels high so people became addicted?

In the afternoon, Cable tried to introduce a lot of details into Krigler's testimony, to confuse the jury. But during coffee, Nicholas explained to them what Cable was doing.

By the end of Thursday, the price of Pynex shares was down. Krigler was quickly flown out of Biloxi by Rohr's security people. Pynex had paid him three hundred thousand dollars out of court just to get rid of him. They wanted him to agree never to testify in trials. He refused, and so his life would always be in danger.

Chapter 6   The Stillwater Bay Development

Millie Dupree's husband, Hoppy, owned a struggling real estate agency in Biloxi. He worked hard with the little business that came his way. Somehow he took care of his family—his wife, Millie, and their five kids.

Just before six on Thursday, a well-dressed young businessman entered the office and asked for Mr. Dupree. His business card showed him to be Todd Ringwald of KLX Property Group, from Las Vegas, Nevada. His company liked to work with smaller companies, he said, and Hoppy had been highly recommended. He showed Hoppy a map.

"MGM Grand is coming here. But no one knows it yet. They're going to build the biggest casino on the Coast. Probably the middle of next year. We want this." On the map he pointed to a large area of land north-west of the proposed casino. Then he showed Hoppy an artist's drawing of the land labeled Stillwater Bay. There were office buildings, big homes, smaller homes, a dock, parks, a shopping mall, even a proposed high school.

"The whole thing will cost thirty million dollars. These are just the first drawings. I'll show you more if you can come to our office in Las Vegas."

Hoppy's knees shook and he took a deep breath. "What kind of help were you thinking about from us?"

"First we need someone to arrange the purchase of the land, then we'll need a real estate firm to advertise and sell the whole development."

"How much will the land cost?" asked Hoppy.

"It's expensive. Five million dollars. But the sellers don't really want to sell, so we have to move in quickly. That's why we need a local agent."

Ringwald watched as Hoppy calculated his normal 6 percent fee on the land sale. Three hundred thousand dollars! Hoppy's heart beat faster. And with the whole Stillwater Bay development, he could be a millionaire in five years.

Ringwald said, "I'm assuming your fee is 8 percent. That's what we normally pay."

"Of course," said Hoppy. His tongue was dry. From three hundred thousand dollars to four hundred thousand—just like that! "Who are the sellers?"

"The property is in the sixth district. And the county supervisor is—"

"Jimmy Hull Moke," Hoppy interrupted.

"You know him?"

"Everyone knows Jimmy Hull Moke. He's been in office for thirty years. Cleverest crook on the Coast. On a local level he controls everything."

"Perhaps we should arrange a meeting with Mr. Moke?"

"Meetings don't work. What Moke wants is cash. Lots of it. In secret."

"He doesn't get caught?" asked Ringwald.

"He's pretty bright. Those of us who work along the Coast know how he operates."

"I think the first step is for you to talk to Mr. Moke."

"I have a clean reputation," said Hoppy. For twenty-five years, he'd worked honestly. He wasn't going to change.

"We don't expect you to get dirty." Ringwald paused. "We have ways of delivering what Mr. Moke wants. You won't have to touch it. In fact, you won't even know when anything happens."

Hoppy liked it! Still, he felt cautious. He said he'd like to think about it.

They chatted some more and said goodbye at eight. After Ringwald had left, Hoppy telephoned KLX. He spoke to Mr. Ringwald's assistant, Madeline, who explained that Mr. Ringwald was out of the office.

So, KLX really did exist.

♦

At 7:40 Thursday night, Lonnie Shaver had a message that George Teaker had called. He rang back and for the first ten minutes answered nothing except questions about the trial. Lonnie confessed that it had been a bad day for the defense, as Lawrence Krigler had made a big impression on all the jurors—all except Lonnie, of course.

Teaker said that the folks in New York were worried. They were relieved that Lonnie was on the jury, and was reliable. He said that they needed to arrange the final details of Lonnie's new contract. He currently earned forty thousand dollars. SuperHouse would give him fifty thousand with some share options and an extra annual payment which might be twenty thousand dollars.

An hour later, Lonnie stood at his window and told himself that he'd soon be earning seventy thousand dollars a year. Not bad for a kid whose father drove a milk truck.

♦

On Thursday night, Hoppy Dupree slept little. The agreement with Jimmy Hull Moke worried him. He'd never before been involved with anything dishonest. He sat on his porch and thought. But just before dawn on Friday morning, he started to feel better. Surely Moke would know how not to get caught. Hoppy wouldn't get near the cash. He decided that he'd have a chat with Moke, and then report to Ringwald.

On Friday morning, the *Wall Street Journal* printed an article about Krigler which said that he hadn't been a satisfactory employee and that there were mistakes in his research. The company denied that tobacco was addictive.

The newspaper also said that Pynex shares had risen, then fallen.

Judge Harkin read the story. He checked with Lou Dell that the jurors couldn't have seen it.

♦

In court, the defense tried to look relaxed for the day after Krigler. It was important that they didn't seem bothered. They wore light-colored suits, and smiled at the jurors.

"Why are they so happy?" whispered one of the jurors.

"They want us to think everything is under control," whispered back Nicholas.

Wendall Rohr called the next witness, Dr. Roger Bunch. He'd become famous ten years earlier, when he'd worked for the government and had been fiercely critical of the tobacco industry. Since leaving office, he'd continued to criticize smoking. He wanted to share his views with the jury. Cigarettes cause lung cancer, and cigarettes are addictive. Tobacco companies spend billions deceiving the public. They spend money on studies which claim that smoking is harmless. Bunch's study showed that cigarettes contain poisonous chemicals, and trash swept off the floor. He had the jury's attention.

♦

Hoppy arranged to meet Jimmy Hull Moke at his office. He'd provided sandwiches and iced tea, but he was too nervous to eat anything himself. He showed Moke the drawing of the Stillwater Bay development and presented the project.

"Who's doing this?" Moke asked.

38

Hoppy had practiced his answer. He couldn't give a name, not at this point.

Moke frowned. "There could be problems with zoning and planning. But, as you know, the supervisors make the final decisions."

"My client is anxious to work with you."

"You know I control everything in my district. If I want this approved, it will be. If I don't like it, it's dead."

Hoppy nodded.

Moke said, "You know, my son is a very fine consultant for projects like this."

"I didn't know that. My client would love to work with your son." Ringwald wanted Hoppy to find out what Moke wanted. "How much might he charge for his services?"

"A hundred thousand dollars." Hoppy didn't show any emotion. KLX had said the deal might cost up to two hundred thousand. "A penny less than that, and I'll kill the deal with one phone call."

"I need to make a phone call," Hoppy said. He walked into the front room and rang Ringwald. He returned to his office. "It's OK," he said slowly. "My client will pay." It felt good to arrange this deal. KLX on one side, Moke on the other, and Hoppy in the middle, with no involvement.

♦

On Friday afternoon, Fitch didn't attend the trial. Instead he continued to study the jury file from the Cimmino case, which he'd received three days earlier. Three hundred possible jurors had received a summons. One of them was a young man called David Lancaster. There was nothing strange in his file, except a note saying that when he appeared on the first day there was no record of his summons being issued. But he was able to show the relevant papers. One of the jury consultants had noticed that Lancaster seemed anxious to be on the jury. However, he wasn't selected.

Fitch had learned that David Lancaster had disappeared from Allentown a month after the trial. By Wednesday night, Fitch was almost certain that David Lancaster was Nicholas Easter.

Carl Nussman, Fitch's chief jury consultant, had looked through the papers of another tobacco trial in Oklahoma. One of the possible jurors there was a young white male called Perry Hirsch. He was almost selected for the jury, but missed it at the last moment. Soon afterward, he left town. Again, no one knew anything about him.

Fitch and his staff stared at the photos of Hirsch, Lancaster, and Easter. The three faces were of the same person. After lunch, a handwriting expert analyzed their writing. He announced without any doubt, "Hirsch and Lancaster are the same people. Hirsch and Easter are the same people. Therefore Lancaster and Easter must be the same."

"All three are the same," said Fitch, slowly.

"That's correct. And he's very, very bright."

♦

Marlee called Fitch late on Friday night in his hotel. No one outside his team knew where he was. The call was put through to the hotel's front desk, but the hotel was being paid a lot of money to protect Fitch's secrecy, so they couldn't admit that he was a guest. When Marlee called again, she was put through to Fitch, on his orders.

"Hi, Fitch. Sorry to call so late."

"No problem," he said. "How's your friend?"

"Lonely. Tonight was the night for jurors' personal visits."

"Why didn't you visit your lover?"

"Who said we're lovers? I tell you, Fitch, Krigler really worked well for the plaintiff. They listened to every word."

"Tell me some good news."

"Rohr's worried."

"What's worrying Rohr?" he asked, looking at his puzzled face in the mirror. He felt betrayed.

"You. He knows you're trying to think up all kinds of ways to get to the jury."

"How often do you talk to him?"

"A lot. He's sweeter than you, Fitch. He doesn't tape my calls or send goons to follow me."

"So Rohr knows how to charm a girl?"

"Yes, but he hasn't got as much money as you."

"How much of my money do you want?"

"Later, Fitch. I must run. There's a suspicious-looking car across the street. It must be some of your goons."

Fitch showered and tried to sleep. At 2 A.M. he drove to the casino. By dawn, he'd won nearly twenty thousand dollars.

Chapter 7   A Fire

The first Saturday in November was unusually cool for the near-tropical climate of the Coast. The jurors, accompanied by Lou Dell and her husband, five part-time deputies, and two other court officials, went by private bus to New Orleans. They shopped at outdoor markets, bought souvenirs, and at four went on a sightseeing trip on a boat.

They were back home at ten, tired and ready for sleep.

♦

Early that same morning, Hoppy was just making coffee when he heard the doorbell. Two young men stood on the doorstep. When Hoppy heard "FBI,"* he nearly fainted.

---

* FBI: the US internal security service.

"Mr. Dupree," Agent Nitchman said when the introductions were completed. "We'd like to ask you some questions."

"About what?" Hoppy asked, his voice dry.

"Questions about Stillwater Bay, Jimmy Hull Moke, things like that," Nitchman explained.

Hoppy grabbed the door, "Oh, my God," he said.

"May we come in?" Agent Napier said.

"No please, not here." The children! "My office, please."

There were no sounds from upstairs. The kids were still sleeping. He dressed fast, and thought about calling Todd Ringwald, or his lawyer. He thought of the public shame. How could he have been so stupid?

Nitchman started. "Are you familiar with Stillwater Bay?"

"Yes."

"Have you met a man by the name of Todd Ringwald?"

"Yes."

"Have you signed any kind of contract with him?"

"No."

"What was the purpose of your meeting with Jimmy Hull Moke?"

"To discuss the development of Stillwater Bay."

Napier cleared his throat. "We've been investigating Mr. Moke for the last six months. We agreed to make things easier for him if he helped us. Did you offer money to Mr. Moke?"

"No," Hoppy said. He hadn't actually offered money. He'd made it possible for his client, Mr. Ringwald, to offer money.

Nitchman took out a pocket tape recorder and put it on the table. "Sure?" he asked. He pressed a button. Hoppy held his breath. Then, there was his voice and then Moke's.

Hoppy stared at the tape recorder, defeated. When he finally looked at them, his eyes were red. "So what will happen to me?"

"For trying to bribe a government official? I'd say three to five years in prison."

The microphone had been hidden in a pen, which was sitting in a jar with other pens and pencils on Hoppy's desk. Ringwald had put it there on Friday morning, when Hoppy had left his office briefly. From the desk, the recording had been sent to a van, recorded onto tape and delivered to Fitch's office. Moke, of course, wasn't involved; he was simply behaving like he always did, trying to make money from bribes. Ringwald, Napier, and Nitchman all worked for a security firm that Fitch often used. The Hoppy scam would cost The Fund eighty thousand dollars, a tiny amount for them.

Hoppy mentioned legal representation. But it was important that Hoppy didn't talk to a lawyer, who'd want names and addresses.

"We know you're not a crook," Nitchman said softly.

"You just made a mistake," added Napier. "Let's keep this quiet for twenty-four hours. We need time to think about your situation. There may be a way out for you, Mr. Dupree. We'll meet here tomorrow at nine o'clock in the morning."

"It's a deal," said Hoppy.

♦

Since the Hoppy scam was going well, Fitch decided to act. Early Sunday morning, Pang and Dubaz, another of Fitch's employees, dressed as workmen, broke into Nicholas's apartment. Dubaz went straight to the camera hidden above the refrigerator, and removed it.

Pang managed to remove the back of the computer and take out what he needed, while Dubaz searched for more computer disks. It didn't take long.

"Let's go," said Pang.

They threw the computer onto the sofa, and covered it with pillows and clothing. Then they poured lighter fuel on top, walked to the door, and Dubaz threw a match onto the heap.

When the flames were near the ceiling, they left quickly, locking the door behind them. Downstairs, they pulled a fire alarm. Then they began banging on the front doors of the other apartments. There were screams as people came out into the hallways.

"Make damn sure you don't kill anyone," Fitch had warned them.

As the crowd went out into the parking lot, Pang and Dubaz separated. When the firemen arrived, they disappeared. No one died and no one was injured. Four apartments were destroyed, eleven badly damaged.

♦

Easter's computer disks were almost impossible to read. They were so secure that Fitch's computer experts were defeated. However, they did manage to read one disk. On it there were current news items about the tobacco industry, information about other legal cases, and a poem about rivers. It was impossible to decide whether Easter was sympathetic to smokers, or just interested in the law.

Finally they found a two-page letter to Easter's mother, a Mrs. Pamela Blanchard, in Gardner, Texas. In it, he apologized for not writing sooner, and said he'd found a job in a casino. Although he still thought about being a lawyer, he doubted he'd ever return to his law studies. He signed the letter *Love Jeff*. Fitch immediately sent two people by private plane to Gardner.

There was one other important piece of information: a list of people registered to vote in Harrison County. From A through K, there were 16,000 names and addresses. The list itself wasn't secret. But two things about it were odd. First, it was on a disk, which meant that somehow Easter had managed to steal the information from a court computer. Second, why did Easter need it?

Fitch knew that Easter was quite capable of altering the list to have his own name entered as a possible juror in the *Wood* v. *Pynex* case.

♦

Hoppy's eyes were red and swollen as he drank coffee at his desk early on Sunday morning. At nine, Napier and Nitchman entered with a third, older man. He was introduced as George Cristano, from Washington, Department of Justice. His handshake was cold.

"Hoppy, could we have this little chat elsewhere?"

They left town in a big black Lincoln Town Car and drove to a dock near Bay St. Louis. Hoppy followed Cristano onto a boat named *Afternoon Delight*.

"Sit down, Hoppy," said Cristano. The boat rocked slightly. Cristano sat opposite Hoppy. "I'll be brief. We have a deal for you which means that you can walk away. No arrest, no trial, and no prison. In fact, Hoppy, no one will ever know."

"I'm listening," interrupted Hoppy.

"This deal has nothing to do with the law. It's political. There'll be no record of it in Washington. Are you worried about crime and drugs, Hoppy?"

"Of course."

"Everything's political these days. We're constantly fighting with the government and with the President. Do you know what we need in Washington? We need more good Republicans who'll give us money and keep out of our way. The Democrats are always talking about budget cuts and the rights of criminals. We have to protect our friends, Hoppy, and you can help us." Cristano paused and looked up and down the dock. He leaned closer. "Your wife can help."

"Millie?"

"It's the trial, Hoppy. Guess who gives most money to Republican candidates? The tobacco companies. They give millions of dollars because they're annoyed by government rules.

They believe people should be free to smoke if they want to. If they lose this trial, there'll be a flood of lawsuits. The companies will lose millions of dollars, and so we'll lose millions of dollars in Washington. Can you help us, Hoppy?"

"Sure, I guess, but how?"

"Talk to your wife and make her see that this case is dangerous. She needs to stand up against the liberals who might want a big verdict for the plaintiff. Can you do that?"

"Of course I can. I'll see her tonight, in fact."

They talked about the best way to persuade Millie. Hoppy asked what would happen if Millie voted with the tobacco company, but the rest of the jury disagreed. Cristano promised that if Millie voted correctly, everything would be all right.

Hoppy almost danced along the dock as he returned to the car. He was a new man.

♦

Judge Harkin wouldn't allow the jurors to go to their different churches on Sunday. Instead, he arranged for a service to be held at the Siesta Motel. At two, relatives started arriving with clean clothes for the jurors. As Easter had no close relatives in the area, Willis drove him to his apartment.

The fire had been out for some hours. The narrow front garden and sidewalk were full of burnt items and wet clothing. Neighbors were cleaning up. Nicholas felt weak at the knees. He walked to the first group of people.

"When did this happen?" he asked.

"This morning, about eight," a woman answered. "Do you live here?"

"Yes, Easter, in 312."

"It's totally destroyed. That's probably where the fire started."

The security guard led Nicholas up the steps to the second

46

floor. There was nothing left of his apartment, except the kitchen wall. No furniture and, to his horror, no computer.

◆

Sunday evening from 6 P.M. was personal visits. Hoppy arrived first and started to talk about the trial to Millie. Nicholas managed to leave the jurors' wing of the motel unnoticed, and went up to the second floor, where Marlee had booked a room.

Marlee and Nicholas had first met in Lawrence, Kansas, where she worked as a waitress and he was at law school. Marlee's mother had died a few years previously and she'd inherited almost two hundred thousand dollars. They fell in love. Nicholas hated studying law, and finally left law school. In their four years together they'd traveled to half a dozen countries. They'd also followed tobacco trials, staying in places such as Allentown, and now, Biloxi. Together they knew more about nicotine, lung cancer, jury selection, and Rankin Fitch than any group of experts.

◆

Rohr spent Sunday evening meeting with the other trial lawyers who'd each given a million dollars toward fighting this case. They were discussing how many more witnesses for the plaintiff should be called. The trial was now three weeks old. Rohr had enough experts to continue for at least two more weeks. Although Cable had his experts, defense witnesses normally took less than half the time of the plaintiff.

However, this tobacco trial was unique because of the sequestered jury, and at some point this jury would rebel. The lawyers argued for an hour. Rohr thought that the jury had heard enough and he wanted to use only two more witnesses. Other lawyers disagreed, quoting evidence from the jury consultants. Rohr felt he could understand the jury better himself.

Chapter 8   Family Backgrounds

Nicholas had a private meeting with Judge Harkin on Monday morning. He assured him that he was fine, in spite of the fire. He was just a student, with little to lose, except a fine computer and some good security equipment.

Since they were alone, Harkin asked him how the other jurors were. It would have been more appropriate if the lawyers had been present. But he could trust this kid.

"Everything's fine," Nicholas said.

"Is the case being discussed?"

"No. When we're together, we try not to talk about it."

"Good, let me know if there's a problem. And let's not talk about this meeting to anyone."

"Sure," said Nicholas. They shook hands and he left.

Rohr's next witness was Leon Robilio. He was led into the courtroom through a side door. A deputy helped him sit down. He was old and pale, dressed in a dark suit, white shirt, and no tie. He had a hole in his throat, covered with a bandage and hidden under a white scarf. When he swore to tell the truth, he did so by holding a pencil-like microphone to his throat. His voice was flat. He was a victim of throat cancer; he'd lost part of his throat eight years earlier, and had learned to talk in this way. He'd smoked heavily for almost forty years and his habit had almost killed him.

The jury quickly became accustomed to Robilio's mechanical voice. He told them that he'd worked for twenty years for the tobacco industry. He'd left the job when he got cancer and when he realized that, even with the disease, he couldn't stop smoking. He was addicted. He still worked full time, but now was fiercely critical of smoking. In his previous job he'd seen a lot of studies of cigarettes and the tobacco industry. He referred to Krigler's evidence.

Robilio regretted many things that he'd done when he

48

promoted the tobacco industry. But he most regretted his denials that the industry aimed its advertising at teenagers. "We spent millions studying kids. We knew that they could name the three most advertised brands of cigarettes. We knew that almost 90 percent of the kids under eighteen who smoked preferred the top three advertised brands. So what did the companies do? They increased the advertising."

"Did you know how much money the tobacco companies were making from cigarette sales to children?" Rohr asked.

"About two hundred million dollars a year. The tobacco companies know that 3,000 kids start smoking every day and that nearly all adult smokers start as teenagers. So they have to target young kids. They know that one-third of the 3,000 kids who start smoking today will die from their addiction."

The jury was fascinated by Robilio.

Rohr took a few steps forward. Then he asked, "How did you answer the arguments that nicotine is addictive?"

"I helped the tobacco companies think of the answer. It goes something like this: 'Smokers choose the habit. So it's a matter of choice. Cigarettes aren't addictive, but, even if they are, no one forces anyone to smoke.' I used to make this argument sound good. The trouble is, it's not true."

"Why isn't it true?"

"Because the issue is addiction and an addict can't make choices. And kids become addicted quicker than adults."

Hoppy came to the trial that Monday morning, for the first time. Millie was thrilled to see him. His sudden interest in the trial was strange, however; he'd talked about nothing else for four hours the night before.

After a coffee break, Cable started to question Robilio for the defense. He started well when Robilio admitted that he was being paid for attending at court. Cable then tried to make Robilio lose his temper. He asked Robilio about his children, who'd all smoked, and reminded him about the work the industry was doing to stop teenagers smoking.

Robilio wasn't persuaded. "The industry will spend a little money to look responsible. But they do that because they know the truth. If they spend two billion dollars next year advertising cigarettes, more young people will become addicted. And you're a fool if you don't believe this."

Judge Harkin leaned forward. "Mr. Robilio, that is unnecessary."

"Sorry, Your Honor. And sorry to you, Mr. Cable. You're just doing your job. It's your client I hate."

"Why?" Cable immediately regretted asking the question.

"Because these tobacco people are clever. They're bright, intelligent, educated, and dishonest. They'll tell you that cigarettes aren't addictive. And they know it's a lie."

"No further questions," said Cable.

♦

Nicholas was silent during lunch. He avoided glances and looked sad. The mood was generally serious. The jurors could still hear Leon Robilio's mechanical voice. Three thousand kids start to smoke each day. One-third of these will die from their addiction.

One of the jurors asked Jerry Fernandez, "How old were you when you started smoking?"

"Fourteen."

"Why did you start?"

"The Marlboro Man." The jurors thought of the image in the advertisement. The cowboy on the horse, the hat, the snow on the mountains behind. Why would a young boy of fourteen not want to be the Marlboro Man?

"Are you addicted?" Rikki Coleman asked Jerry.

"I don't know," he said. "I guess I could stop. I've tried to stop a few times. Sure, it would be nice to stop."

"You don't enjoy it?" Rikki asked.

"Oh, there are times when a cigarette is just what I want, but I smoke two packs a day now, and that's too much."

"I was sixteen when I started," Sylvia admitted.

"I started at fourteen," Herman offered. "Gave up when I was forty."

"Did anybody start smoking after the age of eighteen?"

Not a word.

♦

Nitchman met Hoppy for a sandwich. Hoppy was nervous about being seen in public with an FBI agent, and was relieved when Nitchman arrived wearing jeans. Nitchman handed Hoppy a piece of paper. He said it had just come from Cristano at the Justice Department. In fact, the document had been written by two of Fitch's people.

It was a faxed copy of a report on Leon Robilio. Hoppy read it quickly while eating French fries. Robilio was being paid half a million dollars to testify. He'd been fired from his job for dishonesty, he had a history of mental illness, and his throat cancer was probably the result of his alcohol abuse.

"Really?" Hoppy said, his mouth full of potatoes.

"Mr. Cristano thought you should somehow give this to your wife," Nitchman said. "She should only show it to people she can trust on the jury."

"Right." Hoppy folded the paper and put it in a pocket.

♦

Nicholas's mother, Pamela Blanchard, lived in the old part of Gardner. She was married to the president of a local bank. He wasn't the father of Nicholas or Jeff or whoever he was. She had two sons by a previous marriage which ended in divorce. One was in Alaska, one was a lawyer, or studying to be a lawyer. Something like that.

Fitch's people finally found a college teacher who told them that Jeff Kerr had gone to law school in Kansas. Fitch arranged for a local security firm to start searching Lawrence, Kansas for any trace of Jeff Kerr.

They discovered that Jeff Kerr had registered as a law student, but didn't receive a degree. A local investigator found a lawyer who'd been a student with Jeff and went to see him. The lawyer, Tom Ratliff, said he hadn't seen Jeff in four years. Jeff had left law school because he suddenly hated the idea of being a lawyer. Also, he fell in love.

"Who was the woman?"

"Claire. She worked in a bar, Mulligan's. I heard that he and Claire left town, but I never heard from him again."

Employment records at Mulligan's gave her full name: Claire Clement.

♦

On Monday afternoon in court, an economist gave some information about Jacob Wood's finances. He told the court what Mr. Wood's salary was when he died, and calculated how much his future earnings would have been. One of the defense lawyers tried to challenge the figures. But the lost salary was just the beginning. Rohr would add pain and suffering, medical care, and the price of the funeral.

An hour before the end of the day, Rohr announced his last witness, Mrs. Celeste Wood. The jury hadn't realized that the plaintiff was almost finished. Several of them smiled. Tonight would be their seventh night in sequestration. According to Nicholas's theory, the defense would take no more than three days. They did the math. They could be home by the weekend!

Celeste Wood was fifty-five, thin, with short gray hair. She worked for a library and had brought up three children. She'd practiced what she was going to say and she answered Rohr's questions easily. She talked about her husband, kids, and grandchildren. Her husband had wanted to stop smoking, but he couldn't. The addiction was too strong.

Cable didn't question her. What could he ask?

Judge Harkin looked at his jury. They were tired. "Ladies and gentlemen," he said, "I have good news and bad. The good news is obvious. The plaintiff is calling no more witnesses. The defense has fewer witnesses. The bad news is that the lawyers and I have to deal with other business concerning the trial. We'll have to do that tomorrow, probably all day."

Nicholas raised his hand. "You mean we have to sit around at the motel all day tomorrow?"

"I'm afraid so."

"I don't understand why."

"What do you want to do?"

"We could hire a big boat and go fishing."

"I can't ask the taxpayers to pay for that, Mr. Easter."

"I'm sure that the lawyers wouldn't mind paying."

Rohr answered first, "We'd be happy to pay half."

"It's a great idea, Judge," said Cable loudly.

Nicholas put up his hand again. "Excuse me, Your Honor, maybe some jurors would prefer to shop in New Orleans."

No problem. Rohr and Cable would divide the costs.

◆

Rohr and his team had presented ten witnesses to the jury, including the video of Jacob Wood. It had taken thirteen days. If the jury hadn't been sequestered, Rohr would have called at least three more experts, but he knew it was time to stop. This was no ordinary jury, with a blind man as foreman, at least two strikes, and lists of demands.

The jury didn't seem ordinary to Fitch, either. He had huge experience of influencing juries. Things were going well. Only one fire, and no broken bones. But Marlee had changed everything. With her, he could purchase a verdict. In this, the biggest tobacco trial ever, his lovely Marlee would hand him a verdict. A victory over Rohr in Biloxi would make future litigation much more difficult. It might even save the industry.

When Fitch counted the jury's votes, he thought there were four jurors with him and one that could go either way. Another would probably vote against the tobacco companies. That left Easter and the remaining five, who'd vote with Easter. Nine votes were needed by either side for a verdict, or the trial would have to take place again.

In his office, Rohr was sure that he had nine votes.

Chapter 9   Buying a Verdict

In Lawrence, Kansas, Fitch's local investigator tried too hard. Small spoke to a girl called Rebecca, who'd worked at Mulligan's with Claire Clement. Small went to see her in the bank where she worked.

"Didn't you work with Claire Clement a few years ago?" Small asked.

"Maybe. Who wants to know?"

"Do you know where she is now?"

"No. Why are you asking?"

"Well, she's a possible juror in a trial. My firm has been asked to investigate her background."

"Where's the trial?"

"Can't tell you. You worked at Mulligan's, right?"

"Yes. That was a long time ago."

"Have you talked to her recently?"

"Not in the last four years. Now please, I'm very busy, and you're wasting your time."

When Small had gone, Rebecca rang the number of an apartment in St. Louis, and left a recorded message for her friend, Claire. They chatted at least once a month, though they hadn't seen each other in a year. Claire and Jeff lived an odd life, never staying long in one place. Only the apartment in St. Louis stayed the same. Claire had warned Rebecca that people might come and ask difficult questions. She'd hinted that she and Jeff were working for the government.

When Marlee checked her messages at the St. Louis apartment, she was worried. She called Rebecca and managed to sound perfectly normal, though her mouth was dry. Rebecca was able to remember the whole conversation.

"Are you OK?" Rebecca asked her friend.

"Oh, we're fine," Marlee assured her. They said goodbye to each other, and promised to keep in contact.

Neither Marlee nor Nicholas had believed they'd be traced to Lawrence. Who'd found them? Which side, Fitch or Rohr? More likely Fitch, because he was smarter and had more money. What had been their mistake? How much did these people know? She needed to speak to Nicholas, but he was on a boat with his fellow jurors.

◆

Fitch was in the office when the call came.

"Hello, Marlee," he said to the girl of his dreams.

"Hey, Fitch. What are the chances of a meeting without your goons hiding behind the bushes?"

"The chances are excellent."

"You're lying. Let's do it this way. Let's meet and talk, and if my people see your people, this is the end."

"It's a deal."

"I'm at Casella's, a seafood restaurant at the end of the Biloxi dock. I'm waiting."

When Fitch arrived at the restaurant, Marlee was sitting at a wooden table with an umbrella above it. She was wearing jeans, sunglasses, and a fishing cap.

"I got a call from Lawrence this morning," she said, and Fitch swallowed. "It seems you have some goons up there trying to find things out."

"I don't know what you're talking about." Fitch didn't sound very certain.

So it was Fitch! His eyes betrayed him!

"Right. One more phone call like that, and you'll never hear my voice again." She said nothing for a moment.

"Fine, whatever you want. I just wish I knew what you were talking about," said Fitch. She was silent for a moment. Then finally, Fitch said, "When do we stop playing games?"

"Now."

"Wonderful. How much money do you want?"

"I'll name a price later. It depends on what you want. The jury can do one of four things. It can deliver a verdict for the plaintiff. It can split down the middle, and there will have to be a retrial. It can vote nine to three in your favor and you have a huge victory. It can vote twelve to zero in your favor, and you and your clients can relax for several years."

"I know all this."

"Of course you do. If we forget a verdict for the plaintiff, then you have three choices."

"What can you deliver?"

"Anything I want. Including a verdict for the plaintiff."

"So the other side is willing to pay?"

"We're talking."

"Tell me how the deal works."

"It's very simple. We agree on the verdict you want. Then we agree on the price. You get your money ready. We wait until the lawyers finish their closing arguments, and the jury withdraws to discuss the case. At that moment I give you instructions about which bank you send the money to. When the bank confirms they've received the money, the jury delivers your verdict."

"But there's no guarantee," he protested.

She leaned forward. "Do you doubt me, Fitch?"

Fitch would pay. He'd decided a week earlier to pay whatever she wanted, and he knew that when the money left The Fund there were no guarantees. He didn't care, he trusted his Marlee. He'd love to ask her lots of questions, but he knew she wouldn't answer. He also knew she'd deliver his verdict. She'd worked too hard to fail.

"I'm not totally helpless in this, you know," he said, trying to look in control.

"Of course not, Fitch. I know you've laid traps for at least four of the jurors. Shall I name them?"

No, he didn't want her to name them. How did he know if she was telling the truth? It simply wasn't fair.

"I feel you doubt whether I'm in control. What if I get a juror removed from the jury, say, Lonnie Shaver?"

Fitch tried not to react. "No, he's harmless. I think we should keep Lonnie. But I can't agree a deal without details."

Without any hesitation she said, "And I'm not agreeing to anything as long as you keep investigating my past."

"Are you hiding something?"

"No, but I don't like getting phone calls from my friends. One more call, and I'll never speak to you again."

"Don't say that."

"I mean it, Fitch. Stop your people. If you don't, I'll talk to Rohr. He might want to do a deal. A verdict for him means you have no job, and your clients lose billions. You can't afford it, Fitch." She was right about that. "I'm hungry, " she said. "I'll call you in a couple of days."

"I'm hungry too," he said.

"No thanks, I'll eat alone."

♦

The boat traveled eighty kilometers from the coast, where half the jury started fishing. One of the jurors, Angel Weese, got sick but recovered with the help of some medicine and actually caught the first big fish. Nicholas and Jerry had decided to chat to Lonnie Shaver. Nicholas was friendly with Jerry, who sometimes agreed to say what Nicholas wanted him to. It was a game to him; he had no idea what Nicholas was really doing. They made sure that Lonnie had a supply of cold beer, and after a few cans he talked more easily.

"I wonder how many experts the defense will call," Nicholas said.

"They don't have to call any," Lonnie said, staring at the sea.

"You've had enough?" Nicholas said.

"Damned ridiculous. A man smokes for thirty-five years, then wants millions for his family after he kills himself."

"Jerry and I thought that you would support the defense," Nicholas said.

"And what about you?" Lonnie asked.

"Me, I'm still open-minded. Jerry's leaning toward the defense, because he's addicted to nicotine. He thinks he can stop smoking if he really wants to, so Jacob Wood should have stopped long before he got cancer. Right?"

"That's about right," Jerry said.

The boat returned soon after five. Its arrival was reported to Fitch. He was in his office with one of his people, Swanson, replacing the goons that had annoyed Marlee with another firm who guaranteed not to get caught. Swanson was going to Kansas City to direct operations. Fitch couldn't lose Marlee, but he had to know who she was. There was something hidden in her past.

♦

Angel Weese was in love with and planned to marry Derrick Maples, a young man who was between jobs and between wives. He was in the process of divorcing his first wife. They had two young children, and his wife and her lawyer wanted six hundred dollars a month. The situation wasn't good.

Angel was two months' pregnant, though she'd told no one except Derrick.

Derrick's brother Marvis had once been a deputy sheriff and was now a part-time minister. Marvis was approached by a man named Cleve, who said he'd like to meet Derrick. Introductions were made. Cleve was known as a runner. He ran cases for Wendall Rohr. His usual task was to find good death and injury claims and make sure that they went to Rohr's office. Cleve had to work carefully; looking for clients like this wasn't considered acceptable behavior. On his business card, he was called an "Investigator."

Over a beer, Cleve talked to Derrick and quickly realized that he had financial problems. He started asking questions about Angel and the trial.

"Why don't you tell me what this is about?" Derrick asked.

"My client is willing to purchase influence. For cash. Five thousand dollars. Half now, half after the trial."

Derrick smiled. "And I do what?"

"You talk with Angel when you see her during personal visits and you make sure she knows how important this case is to the plaintiff. Just don't tell her about the money, or about me, or any of this. Not now. Maybe later."

"Why not?"

"Because this is illegal, OK? If the Judge found out that I was talking to you, offering you money to talk to Angel, then both of us would go to jail. Understand?"

"Ten thousand. Five now, five when the trial is over."

"OK, ten."

59

◆

Durwood Cable was in charge of keeping D. Martin Jankle away from any alcohol. Fitch and Jankle had fought over the question of whether or not Jankle could drink on the night before he testified. Fitch accused Jankle of having a drink problem. Jankle cursed Fitch for trying to tell him, the CEO of Pynex, if, when, and how much he could drink.

Cable got involved in the argument. He insisted that Jankle stay in his office to prepare his testimony, and then practice it. Jankle performed adequately. Nothing special. Cable made him watch a video of his performance. When he was finally taken to his hotel after ten, he found that Fitch had replaced the alcoholic drinks in his room with juices. He cursed and went to his overnight bag, where he kept a bottle hidden in a leather case. Fitch had removed that too.

◆

At 1 A.M. Nicholas silently opened his motel room door and looked up and down the hall. The guard was gone, probably asleep. Marlee was waiting in a room on the second floor. They kissed. She hurriedly told him about her chat with Rebecca in Lawrence, then she tried to recall every word of her conversation with Fitch.

They were both shocked to realize that they'd been partly discovered. They were sure it was Fitch, and they wondered how much he knew. They were certain that Jeff Kerr would have to be discovered in order to find Claire Clement. Although Jeff's background was harmless, Claire's had to be protected, or they wouldn't be able to continue with their plan.

There was little that they could do except wait.

◆

Derrick entered Angel's room through the window. He couldn't wait until tomorrow night, he told her, because he loved her and missed her. She noticed he'd been drinking.

They awoke at dawn, and Angel was nervous because she had a man in her room and this was against the Judge's orders. Derrick wasn't worried. He'd been thinking and he'd decided that Angel's vote was worth a lot more than ten thousand dollars. He'd suggest to Cleve that they paid him cash now, and then a percentage of the money granted to the plaintiff after the verdict. There would never be a chance like this for him again.

Chapter 10   The Case for the Defense

On Wednesday morning, an analyst named Walter Barker wrote in an article in *Mogul*, a popular weekly financial magazine, that the jury would decide against Pynex and that the sum of money Pynex would have to pay out would be enormous. His opinions were listened to, and he was usually right. Wall Street was shocked. The share price dropped from seventy-six to seventy-one and a half.

The jury arrived in court at nine. Harkin welcomed them, went through his normal questions, and then promised that there would be a speedy end to the trial.

Jankle was called as a witness, and the defense began. Free from the effects of alcohol, Jankle was ready. He smiled and seemed to welcome the chance to defend his tobacco company. Sitting on the second row was Taunton, the black lawyer whom Lonnie had met in Charlotte. It didn't take long for their eyes to meet. Lonnie managed to nod and smile, because it seemed like the polite thing to do. Taunton's message was clear. The defense was speaking, and it was important for Lonnie to understand that he should believe every word that was said by the witness. No problem with Lonnie.

Jankle described the different brands of cigarettes his company made, showing the jury a colorful chart of the eight brands, each with the nicotine levels labeled beside it. By offering this wide selection of brands, Pynex allowed each person to decide how much nicotine he or she wanted. Choose the number of cigarettes you smoke each day. Choose what you do to your body with cigarettes. The message was choice, choice, choice. Cigarettes were responsible products if used carefully. However, like many other products—alcohol, butter, sugar, and handguns, for example—they could become dangerous if they were abused.

Fitch watched all of Jankle's testimony from a seat near the back. To his right was Luther Vandemeer, CEO of Trellco, the largest tobacco company in the world, and the unofficial head of the Big Four. Fitch and Vandemeer had lunch at Mahoney's, alone. They were relieved by Jankle's success that morning, but they knew the trial would become more difficult.

"How much influence do you have with the jury?" asked Vandemeer.

Fitch wasn't going to answer truthfully. He wasn't expected to. No one knew some of the things he did, except his own agents.

"The usual."

"Maybe the usual is not enough." Vandemeer was scared, with good reason. The pressure was enormous. A large plaintiff's verdict would mean an immediate 20 percent loss in shareholder value, and that was just the beginning. There could be one million lung cancer lawsuits during the five years after such a verdict. The legal fees would average one million dollars for each case. Nobody dared predict the cost of one million verdicts. The government might try to ban cigarettes.

"Do you have enough money?" Vandemeer asked.

"I think so," answered Fitch, wondering for the hundredth time how much his dear Marlee might want.

"The Fund should have a lot of money."

"It does."

Vandemeer chewed on a tiny piece of grilled chicken. "Why don't you choose nine jurors and give them a million dollars each?" he said with a little laugh, as if he was joking.

"Believe me, I've thought about it. It's just too risky. People would go to jail."

Vandemeer stopped smiling. "We have to win, Rankin, you understand? We have to win. Spend whatever it takes."

♦

With a jury exhausted by sequestration, Durwood Cable didn't want to extend the case. He'd cut his list of witnesses to five, and he'd planned for their testimony to run for no more than four days.

In the afternoon, Jankle was questioned by Wendall Rohr. Rohr started with a vicious question, and things went from bad to worse.

"Isn't it true, Mr. Jankle, that your company spends hundreds of millions of dollars trying to persuade people to smoke, but when they get sick, your company won't pay a dime to help them?"

Jankle said something that no one could hear.

"I'm sorry, Mr. Jankle. I didn't hear that. When was the last time—"

"I heard the question. I can't recall one."

"So you say that cigarettes don't cause sickness?"

"Only if they're abused."

"So tell us please, Mr. Jankle, how does one abuse a cigarette?"

"By smoking too much."

"And how much is too much?"

"I'd say more than two packs a day."

Rohr spoke more softly. "Will you describe to the jury how

63

you have warned the public that smoking more than forty cigarettes a day is dangerous?"

The damage was done, but Rohr saved the best moment until the end. He showed a video of Jankle, together with the other CEOs, giving evidence before a group of politicians. One by one they were asked if nicotine was addictive. They all clearly said no. Jankle was last, and when he made his angry denial, the jury knew he was lying.

♦

Fitch and Cable had a tense meeting. Fitch was bothered about Jankle's defense. Cable, who didn't like being criticized by a non-lawyer, whom he hated anyway, explained that they'd begged Jankle not to talk about cigarette abuse.

Fitch thought the jury might be tired of Cable. Why couldn't another defense lawyer talk to a few witnesses? There were a lot of them. Fitch and Cable shouted at each other across a desk. After they'd both tried to become calmer, they did agree that the defense should be brief, and last no more than three days. Fitch banged the door shut as he left the office.

In his car, Fitch read faxes. There was a summary of the investigations into Claire Clement in Kansas. The car went past a store, and Fitch suddenly wanted a beer. He was an ex-alcoholic and hadn't had a drink for nine years. He knew that if he had one drink, he'd go on drinking. He stopped thinking about beer. Where was Marlee, and why hadn't she called? He closed his eyes, thought of the jurors, and dreamed of Marlee.

♦

Derrick chose a different place for his meeting with Cleve. It was a bar in the black section of Biloxi. Cleve insisted that they meet in the parking lot first. He arrived late.

"I don't think this is a good idea," Cleve said. "I'm the only white face here, and you expect me to go into the bar with five thousand dollars and hand it over to you? If you want the money, meet me at the Waffle House."

Sitting in the Waffle House, they drank coffee. Derrick was nervous as he spoke.

"So I'm thinking that ten thousand dollars isn't enough, know what I mean?"

"I thought we had a deal," said Cleve, showing no emotion.

"Things are different now. I want fifty thousand dollars, plus a percentage of the sum of money that the plaintiff gets. I think 10 percent would be fair."

"Oh, you do? You're crazy. We made a deal for ten thousand. Anything larger and we'll be caught." Cleve got up and hurried out to the parking lot.

Derrick ran after him and caught up with Cleve in his car. Cleve got out, lit a cigarette, and looked at Derrick.

"Look, what I'm offering you is illegal. Don't get greedy. If you do, you'll be caught."

"But if you offer a percentage, Angel will work harder to persuade the other jurors to decide on a large sum of money."

"You don't understand. If there's a verdict for the plaintiff, it'll be years before the money is actually paid. Take the money. Talk to Angel."

"Twenty-five thousand. Per vote."

"Per vote?"

"Sure. Angel can deliver more than one."

Cleve finished his cigarette. "I'll have to talk to my boss."

♦

It was time for personal visits at the Siesta Motel. Hoppy had arrived early with some Chinese food and a bottle of wine. He and Millie made love, and then talked about the kids. Hoppy spoke sadly about her absence. Everyone missed her.

He dressed and turned on the television. "You're not going to believe this," he said, taking a piece of paper out of his pocket.

"What is it?" said Millie, taking the paper and reading it. It was a copy of the document which Fitch's people had written, with false information about Leon Robilio. Millie looked suspiciously at her husband. "Where did you get this?" she demanded. "Who sent it?"

"Don't know. Looks like it came from Washington." Hoppy hated lying to Millie, but Napier and Nitchman were out there somewhere, just waiting.

"Why didn't you just throw it away?"

"I don't know, I—"

"You know it's wrong to show me stuff like this, Hoppy." Millie threw the paper on the bed and walked closer to her husband. "What are you trying to do?"

"Nothing. Somebody just faxed it to my office, that's all."

"What? Somebody knew your fax number, knew that your wife was on the jury, knew that Leon Robilio testified? And that person also thought that you'd be stupid enough to try to influence me? I want to know what's going on."

"Nothing, I swear," said Hoppy.

"Why have you taken such a sudden interest in the case? I can tell when something's bothering you, Hoppy."

"Nothing. Relax. This case is difficult for both of us. I'm sorry I showed you it."

Millie finished the wine and sat on the bed. Hoppy sat next to her. Mr. Cristano had suggested that Millie showed the document to all of her friends on the jury. Hoppy didn't know how to tell Mr. Cristano that this wouldn't happen. As he thought about this, Millie started crying. "I want to go home," she said, with red eyes.

Hoppy put his arm round her and squeezed tightly. "I'm sorry," he said. She cried even harder.

Hoppy felt like crying too. The meeting hadn't been successful. The trial would end soon. He had to persuade Millie to vote for a defense verdict. Hoppy would be forced to tell Millie the truth. Not tonight, but surely during the next personal visit.

Chapter 11   A Juror's Dismissal

Colonel Herrera's routine never varied. He got up at exactly five-thirty, did his exercises, and took a cold shower. At six he had breakfast in the motel dining room. At eight, he returned to his room.

At 6:15 on Thursday morning, Nicholas greeted the Colonel in the dining room, and had a brief conversation about the weather. He then went quietly down the hall, took a pile of newspapers from a drawer in his room, and used a key he'd stolen from the front desk to enter the Colonel's room. He put the pile of newspapers and magazines under the Colonel's bed. One was a copy of yesterday's *Mogul*. He went to his room and phoned Marlee.

Marlee called Fitch. "Hey, Fitch. Go to the middle pay phone at the corner of Fourteenth and Beach Drive. I'll call in seven minutes."

"Damn it!" Fitch screamed. He shouted for José and they rushed to his car. The phone was ringing as they got there.

"Hey, Fitch. Juror number seven, Herrera, is really annoying Nick. I think we'll lose him today."

"Don't do it, Marlee! He's on our side."

"Oh, Fitch, they'll all be on our side when it's over. Anyway, be in court at nine to see what happens."

Fitch controlled himself, and walked calmly to the car. Whatever she wanted. It didn't matter.

♦

Judge Harkin lived in Gulfport, fifteen minutes from the courthouse. As he was getting ready to leave for the courthouse, the phone rang.

"Judge, I'm sorry to bother you at home," said a nervous voice. "It's Nicholas Easter."

"What's the matter?" The Judge wondered how Nicholas had obtained his phone number, but said nothing.

"It's about Herrera," Nicholas said. "I think maybe he's reading things that aren't on the approved list. This morning, when I went into the dining room, he was there alone and he tried to hide a copy of *Mogul* from me. Isn't that some kind of business magazine?"

"Yes it is," replied Harkin. If Easter was telling the truth, and why should he doubt him, then Herrera would be sent home immediately. The reading of any unauthorized material meant dismissal. "Do you think he's discussed it with anyone else?"

"I doubt it. Like I said, he was trying to hide it from me. But I'll listen carefully."

"You do that. I'll ask Colonel Herrera to come in and see me this morning. We'll probably search his room."

"Please don't tell him I reported him. I feel really bad about doing it."

"It's OK. The trial's almost over, Nicholas. I'm asking the lawyers to be as quick as they possibly can."

On his way to the court, Harkin called the Sheriff and asked him to go to the Siesta Motel and wait. He then called Lou Dell, who told him that *Mogul* wasn't sold at the motel. He wondered how a sequestered juror could have got a copy of it.

When Harkin arrived in court he told Rohr and Cable what he'd learned, without telling them who'd told him. Both lawyers were unhappy. Cable was annoyed because everyone thought that Herrera would vote with the defense. Rohr was cross because they were going to lose a juror, and there was a danger the trial might have to be repeated.

Herrera was called to the Judge's chambers, where he was told he had to answer some questions. He felt like a criminal.

"Have you been reading any materials not specifically authorized by me, in particular a business weekly magazine called *Mogul*?" asked the Judge.

"Not since I've been sequestered," Herrera replied.

"Will you agree to a search of your room?"

The Colonel went red. "What are you talking about?" he demanded.

"I have reason to believe that you have been reading unauthorized materials at the motel. I think a search of your room would settle the matter," replied the Judge.

Herrera knew there was nothing in his room. "Then search it," he said, between his teeth.

In the motel, the Sheriff and two deputies found the newspapers and magazines under Herrera's bed. They took them to the Judge's chambers. The Judge showed them to Herrera. "These items were found under the bed in Room 50, just minutes ago."

Herrera was speechless. "They're not mine," he said angrily. "Somebody must have put them there."

"The fact is that these were found in your room. I have no choice. You are dismissed from jury service."

There were many questions Herrera wanted to ask, but he suddenly realized he'd be on the golf course by lunchtime. "Whatever you say, Judge."

◆

The jurors took their seats a few minutes after ten. In the courtroom, the jury watched silently as Judge Harkin showed them a copy of *Mogul*. He asked if anyone had read it, or heard what was in it. No one.

"Juror number seven, Frank Herrera, has been dismissed and replaced by the extra juror, Mr. Henry Vu."

Fitch's newspaper dropped several inches, as he stared at the new juror. He was scared because Herrera had gone, and thrilled because his girl Marlee had done exactly what she'd promised. Fitch looked at Easter, who stared back.

Cable's first witness on Thursday was Dr. Denise McQuade. The defense wanted to answer Leon Robilio's claims that kids were targeted by the cigarette industry. Dr. McQuade was beautiful and clever. She'd written four books and many articles. She quickly made her point. Advertising is everywhere. Children are familiar with commercials for all kinds of things that kids eat and drink, like hamburgers and soft drinks. No one accuses those companies of dishonestly targeting the young.

Dr. McQuade's testimony made perfect sense to the jury.

◆

Rohr spent his lunch hour with Cleve, discussing what they should do about Derrick. "This is what we'll do," said Rohr. "We'll give him fifteen thousand dollars now, and the other ten after the verdict. We'll promise him twenty-five thousand for the other votes. We'll also record the interview. If we get our verdict, we won't pay, and if he causes problems, we'll threaten to call in the FBI."

"I like it," Cleve said.

"Get the cash. You must see him this afternoon."

Cleve met him in a cheap bar. But Derrick had other plans. He wanted Angel's twenty-five thousand dollars in cash, now, and he also wanted an advance payment for each of the other jurors. Eighty thousand dollars in cash, now.

"You're crazy," Cleve said.

"And you're a crook," replied Derrick.

"There's no way we can pay eighty thousand cash."

"Fine, I'll go to the tobacco company."

"You do that," said Cleve.

♦

On Thursday morning, the search for Claire had a small success. They got information about another friend of Claire's. Her name was Beverly Monk and she lived in Greenwich Village in New York. Swanson flew to New York and phoned her, pretending to be Nicholas. He'd practiced imitating Nicholas's voice many times.

"It's Jeff Kerr."

"Oh yes." Maybe she remembered him, maybe she didn't.

"I'm in the city and I wondered if you'd heard from Claire recently. I'm looking for her."

"I haven't talked to Claire in four years. Look, I'm real busy now."

"Sure." Swanson called Fitch. They decided to offer Beverly Monk cash.

♦

Fitch knew Marlee would ring on Friday morning.

"Hi, Fitch. Lonnie Shaver's bothering Nicholas."

"Oh! Damn! No! You can't do that! You've got to stop this, Marlee." Fitch was aware of how desperate he sounded. "Don't do it, please. Let's talk about this."

"We'll meet in an hour. Fulton Street, number 120."

Fitch walked to Fulton Street. He went alone.

"Are we ready to talk money?" he asked, with a nasty grin.

"Yes. You send me ten million dollars before the verdict."

"You must be joking."

She never stopped looking at him. "Ten million, Fitch, and there's no discussion. How much is in The Fund?"

"The what?" he said. No one knew about The Fund!

"Don't play games, Fitch. I want ten million dollars sent to a bank in Singapore before the jury withdraws to discuss their verdict. Otherwise, the deal's off."

"What happens if the deal's off?"

"One of two things. Either Nicholas will split the jury, or he'll persuade it to vote nine votes to three for the plaintiff." The game was over. She was in control. "So we have a deal?"

"Yes," said Fitch. They shook hands.

♦

Swanson approached Beverly Monk in a corner coffee shop. "Excuse me, are you Beverly Monk?"

She looked up, surprised, and said, "Yes, who are you?"

"A friend of Claire Clement's."

"What do you want?" She was nervous, but the shop was crowded. "You called me yesterday, didn't you?"

"Yes, I did. I lied. I said I was Jeff Kerr. I'm not. I'm Jack Swanson. I work for some lawyers in Washington."

"Is Claire in trouble?"

"No." Swanson gave a quick explanation of Claire's summons to jury service for a huge trial in the future. "We'll pay for information," he said.

"How much?"

"A thousand dollars, cash, to tell me everything you know about Claire Clement." Swanson took out an envelope and placed it on the table. Beverly stared at it, then grabbed it and put it in her purse.

"There's not much to tell," she said. " I worked with her for six months. Then I left town. I called her once or twice, then we lost contact."

"Where did she go to college?"

"Somewhere in the Midwest. Claire was a very secretive person. She didn't talk about her past. I didn't ask."

Swanson thanked her. As he was leaving, she offered to make a few phone calls. She obviously wanted more money. Swanson said fine, and gave her his business card.

◆

Hoppy sat in the back of a long, black Chrysler car with Mr. Cristano. Nitchman and Napier were in the front. Hoppy had met with Nitchman and Napier the day before, and admitted that Millie hadn't reacted too well to the document.

"When do you see her again?" Cristano asked.

"Tonight, I think."

"The time has come, Hoppy, for you to tell her the truth."

Hoppy's eyes watered as he stared out the window. He cursed himself for his stupidity. If he had a gun, he could almost shoot Todd Ringwald and Jimmy Hull Moke. He could definitely shoot himself.

"I guess so," he whispered.

"You'll have to tell her that if she doesn't support the defense's case, you will go to prison for five years."

Hoppy started crying. In the front, Nitchman grinned.

Chapter 12   Hoppy Dupree's Confession

Fitch met with Marlee an hour after the previous meeting ended. "How much does Rohr know?" he asked.

"He knows nothing. We never met. I made you think I'd met him, but it never happened."

"Promise me you won't get rid of Lonnie Shaver," Fitch said.

"Tell me why. If we're working for the same verdict, then we have to be honest."

"All I can say is that Lonnie has been bought and paid for. How many votes does Nicholas have now?"

"He'll have nine votes before the jury withdraws, maybe more. He just needs a bit of help with a few, like Rikki Coleman, for instance."

73

"We might have some information about her."

"You keep playing games, so will I. What about Millie Dupree?" Nicholas had noticed Hoppy's sudden interest in the trial, and he and Marlee had their suspicions that Fitch was trying to use Hoppy to persuade Millie.

Fitch decided to be cautious. "Nothing on Millie," he said.

They discussed the other jurors briefly. Marlee asked for another twenty-five thousand dollars to bribe Jerry Fernandez and another juror, then gave new instructions for the transfer of the ten million dollars. The meeting was over.

Later on Friday, Fitch instructed each of the Big Four CEOs to send two million dollars each to The Fund immediately. There was no time for explanations. He then transferred ten million dollars from The Fund's bank account to a new account which he opened in the Netherlands Antilles. By Friday evening, it was all done. At first, Fitch was relieved, but he knew his work wasn't finished. He didn't know the real Marlee, and why she was doing this. Fitch didn't like the unknown. He soon became angry and worried again.

◆

At eight on Friday evening, Derrick went to Durwood Cable's office. He was nervous and when he asked for a Mr. Gable by mistake, he was told that no one of that name worked there.

◆

In court, Judge Harkin was worried about the jury. It was five on Friday. They were bored and tired. The lawyers were worried too; the jurors weren't reacting to testimony as they should be. They were staring blankly into space or trying to stay awake.

Nicholas wanted the jurors to be tired. They'd listen to him more willingly. He persuaded all the jurors to sign a letter to Judge Harkin asking for the trial to continue on Saturday. Judge

Harkin agreed. "The trial should be over Monday afternoon," he said. "We'll have closing arguments on Monday morning, and you'll receive the case before noon. That's the best I can do."

There were smiles from the jury. With the end in sight, they could manage one more weekend together. There would be personal visits tonight, tomorrow night, and Sunday.

♦

Hoppy arrived in Millie's room late. He sat on her bed and put his face in his hands.

"What's the matter, Hoppy?" she asked, frightened. He finally told her. Mr. Todd Ringwald, Stillwater Bay, Jimmy Hull Moke, Napier, Nitchman, and the tape. How could he have been so stupid! Millie began crying. But there was more. When he got to the part where he did a deal with Mr. Cristano, Millie stopped crying.

"But I'm not sure I want to vote for the tobacco company," she said.

"Wake up, Millie. If you don't, I go to prison for five years."

"That's not fair." Millie was shocked.

"What about the kids?" Hoppy asked. He'd planned his arguments in advance. Millie felt she'd been hit by a bus.

"It's not fair to the people in the trial," she said.

"I know, honey," he replied. "I know. I'm a total failure. Believe me, I've even thought about shooting myself."

"Don't be silly," she said, and started to cry again.

After Hoppy had left, Millie couldn't sleep. At midnight, she went down to the Party Room for a snack. She found Nicholas alone.

"Why are you up so late?" he asked. "You look troubled."

"I am. Can you help me, Nicholas?"

"I'll try."

She told him everything. Nicholas suspected a scam but didn't tell Millie that. She promised to do nothing until they spoke again. He went to his room and rang Marlee.

◆

In court on Saturday, Cable decided to start with a bit of action. His witness was a Dr. Olney, who'd done research on laboratory mice. He had a video of the mice. Over some years the mice had been given huge doses of cigarette smoke. Not one had developed lung cancer.

Hoppy was in court, listening. He'd promised Millie that he'd come to show his support. Derrick sat at the back and continued to plot. Rikki Coleman's husband was also in court; so were the families of some of the other jurors.

◆

Marlee had been working since six on Saturday morning. She called newspaper reporters, the police, FBI information lines, and government information services. She soon decided that the whole Hoppy affair was a scam arranged by Fitch.

Fitch arrived for a meeting with Marlee at ten. Earlier that morning, he'd received a report on the investigations into Claire Clement. Before she arrived in Lawrence in the summer of 1988, she hadn't existed. While in Lawrence, she made no long distance phone calls. After she left Lawrence, the trail led nowhere. She'd probably changed her identity. Whoever she was, she was smart.

"We've got problems with Rikki Coleman," said Marlee. "Nicholas thinks she wants a big verdict."

Without comment, Fitch handed Marlee a piece of paper.

"So she was pregnant? You're sure this is her?"

"Positive."

"You have nothing on Herman Grimes?"

"Nothing," replied Fitch. "Nicholas will have to deal with

him. He's getting paid for it. If there's a problem, can't you get him removed?"

"We're thinking about it."

Fitch shook his head in amazement. "Do you realize what you're doing."

"I think so. That's all for now, Fitch. I have work to do."

Later that day, Marlee received a call from an FBI Agent in Biloxi called Madden. He confirmed that Nitchman, Napier, and Cristano weren't FBI agents and he'd love to talk to them. Marlee said she'd try to arrange a meeting.

♦

At three on Saturday afternoon, the defense finished. The jurors were free to go. There would be trips to a football match or movie theater arranged for Saturday night, followed by personal visits. On Sunday the jurors could go to church, and in the evening there would be more personal visits.

Millie had no interest in movies, and certainly none in football. Hoppy arrived with some food, which they ate slowly. After dinner, they talked about their problems again. There were more tears and more apologies. Finally, Millie confessed that she'd told Nicholas everything. He could be trusted, she said.

At ten-thirty, Nicholas, back from the football game, visited Millie's room. He explained to Hoppy and Millie that the whole thing was a scam. A close friend had made phone calls which confirmed that Napier, Nitchman, and Cristano weren't government agents and that KLX Property Group didn't exist. Hoppy had been tricked. At first Hoppy felt even more stupid, then he had questions. What did it mean? Was it good news or bad? "What about the tape," he asked, "of me and Jimmy Hull Moke?"

"I'm not worried about it," Nicholas said confidently. "The tape was obtained illegally. Forget it."

What sweet words. "You're serious?"

"Yes, Hoppy. The tape will never be played again."

Millie leaned over and kissed Hoppy. This time her tears were of joy.

◆

On Sunday morning, some of the jurors went to church. Hoppy went to his office at ten. He'd called Napier at eight on Sunday morning with the news that he had important developments to discuss; he said he'd managed to persuade his wife, and she was influencing other jurors. Napier called Cristano, who called Fitch. Fitch was delighted and authorized the meeting.

Napier and Nitchman arrived in Hoppy's office at eleven. Hoppy was making coffee. He started talking to his visitors. Another guest quietly entered the building through the front door, which Hoppy had left unlocked. He knocked on Hoppy's door and opened it.

"Agent Alan Madden, FBI," he said, showing his badge. Napier and Nitchman went pale as their hearts stopped.

"The FBI is already here," said Hoppy, acting perfectly, looking at Madden, then the other two, then Madden. "You guys don't know each other?"

"FBI?" Madden said. "Show me your identification."

"I can explain," Nitchman said, his voice higher than normal. "You see we're not really FBI agents—we're private investigators and, well—"

"What!" screamed Hoppy. "You've been telling me for ten days that you're FBI agents. What's going on here?"

"Who *are* you?" Madden asked the two men. There was no response. He took out a gun and searched them. Then he led them from the building, where another FBI agent was waiting. They got into a car and drove away.

In the car, Napier and Nitchman invented a story. They'd been hired to investigate some real estate. One thing led to another, and their boss had made them pretend to be FBI agents. No harm done, really. Madden was a young agent and thought it was a minor crime. He gave them a lecture about pretending to be FBI officers, and told them to stay out of Mississippi.

When Fitch heard the story, he was so angry that he broke a lamp. He sent Pang to fetch the two men. Three hours later Napier and Nitchman were sitting in a room next to Fitch's office, with Cristano.

"Start at the beginning," he said. "I want to hear every word." They remembered nearly everything.

After they'd left, Fitch sat and thought. Hoppy would tell Millie tonight. Millie would be lost as a defense juror. In fact, she would probably go right over to the other side and want billions of dollars for the poor widow Wood.

Marlee could rescue the situation, only Marlee.

Chapter 13   Closing Speeches

Beverly Monk had some information. She'd managed to trace a friend of Claire's, Phoebe. When she called Phoebe, she found out that Phoebe had also received a call from someone pretending to be Jeff Kerr. She knew it wasn't, but had spoken to him anyway. She hadn't seen Claire Clement in four years. Beverly told Phoebe that she wanted to contact Claire again. Phoebe told her Claire's real name.

"It was Brant. Gabrielle Brant. She was from Columbia, Missouri. She had a boyfriend who was crazy and so she changed her name and left town. I think her father's dead. Her mother was a professor at the local university."

"Is she still there?"

"I have no idea."

"I'll try to find her through her mom. Thanks, Phoebe."

Beverly took an hour trying to reach Swanson on the phone to sell him this information. After checking with Fitch, Swanson offered her two and half thousand dollars. They bargained for ten minutes, and finally settled on four thousand, in cash. Swanson immediately flew to New York, arrived at dusk, and called Beverly's roommate, who told him that she might be at a party. He called the pizzeria where she worked, and was told she'd been dismissed. He drank coffee, made phone calls, and waited.

◆

Marlee wanted one more meeting with Fitch. Fitch could have kissed her feet when he saw her.

He decided to tell her everything about Hoppy and Millie and the scam which had gone wrong. Nicholas must talk to Millie immediately, before she spoke to the other jurors. What would she do when she learned the truth? It would be a disaster, no question about it.

Marlee listened without reacting as Fitch told the story. It amused her to see Fitch sweat.

"I think we should get her off the jury," Fitch declared, when he was finished.

"Relax, Fitch. Nicholas and Millie are quite close. Millie will vote the way he wants."

Fitch tried to smile. "Just out of curiosity, how many votes do we have right now?"

"Nine. Look, Fitch, you're worrying too much. You've paid your money, you've got the best, now relax and wait for your verdict. It's in very good hands."

"Will we get all twelve?"

"Nicholas is determined to get them all."

Out of the building, Fitch was almost dancing. José had never seen his boss so happy.

◆

Wendall Rohr and Durwood Cable were each practicing their closing speeches. In a conference room, in front of seven lawyers, Wendall Rohr walked forward and back, speaking softly, with carefully chosen words, to his jury. His voice was warm and rich, filled with sympathy one minute and hard words for the tobacco companies the next. He lectured and persuaded. He was funny, and he was angry. He finished in fifty-one minutes. The closing speech had to be an hour or less—Judge Harkin's orders. The comments from his audience were tough. Rohr agreed to perform again. It had to be perfect. Victory was so close.

Cable had a larger audience. He was videotaped, so he could watch himself. He was determined to do it in half an hour. The jury would like that. Rohr would no doubt go on for longer. Cable delivered his closing speech, then watched the video. Again and again, throughout Sunday afternoon, and into the night.

◆

By the time Fitch arrived at the beach house, he was his normal pessimistic self again. The four CEOs were waiting, having just finished a fine meal. Jankle was drunk. Fitch was questioned about the two million dollars he'd required from each of them. He explained that the defense had a very large, unplanned expense.

"Do you have the votes, Fitch?" asked one of the CEOs.

"I believe I do. The verdict has been purchased." His voice held a touch of pride.

"How?"

"I'll never tell," Fitch said coolly. "The details are not important."

They stared at him. Eight times they'd been to the edge of disaster, and each time Rankin Fitch had saved them. Now he'd done it again. "How much?" Jankle demanded.

"Ten million. I've purchased the verdict for ten million dollars. That's all I'll say. Of course, nothing is guaranteed. You never know until the jury comes back."

Well, it ought to be guaranteed, at a price of ten million dollars. But the CEOs said nothing.

◆

There was a general feeling among the jurors that Sunday night would be their last in sequestration. The mood was more relaxed, and many of the jurors packed up their things. It was the third night of personal visits. Marlee and Nicholas ate pizza in his room and discussed their plans.

Marlee left at nine. Nicholas went to see Hoppy and Millie. They were full of thanks. Millie was worried about staying on the jury. She'd discussed it with Hoppy and didn't feel she could be fair after what had happened. Nicholas had anticipated this and wanted Millie to stay on the jury. If she told Judge Harkin what had happened, then the Judge would probably order the trial to be held again.

"It's our job, Millie," Nicholas said. "We've been chosen to decide this case. It's our responsibility to reach a verdict."

Millie agreed. Her new friend Nicholas made everything easier.

◆

After failing to meet with Cable, Derrick had to deal with Cleve. They met in the Nugget Casino on Sunday night, and drank a beer. Cleve gave Derrick a packet containing fifteen thousand dollars. The other ten thousand would be paid after the verdict, as long as Angel voted for the plaintiff.

After Cleve had left, Derrick stayed behind to gamble. He bet heavily. The beers kept coming. Down to seven thousand dollars. He wanted to cry. But his luck changed, and he left the casino with nearly eleven thousand dollars.

Although it was too late for personal visits, he got in his car and started to drive to the Siesta Motel. Soon he noticed blue lights behind him. He stopped the car.

"Have you been drinking?" asked a policeman. Derrick was taken to jail. A five-hour stay was automatic for drunk drivers. He couldn't phone Angel from jail, but he had to reach her before she left for court.

At five-thirty on Monday morning, Marvis arrived at the police station to collect Derrick. Derrick gave his brother two hundred dollars, and borrowed his car. He raced to the Siesta Motel and tried to wake Angel by throwing stones at her window.

"Don't move!" said a voice behind him. Derrick turned to see Chuck, one of the deputies, with a gun. "Hands up."

Derrick was taken to jail for the second time that night.

Angel slept through it all.

♦

On Monday morning, while Nicholas helped Mrs. Grimes prepare Herman's breakfast, he dropped four small tablets into Herman's coffee. They wouldn't kill him. Herman would be sick for four hours, then recover completely.

Nicholas carried their breakfast back to the Grimes's room. Mrs. Grimes thanked him; such a nice young man.

The drama started half an hour later. The door to the Grimes's room was open and Herman was bent double on the bathroom floor. Lou Dell ran to the phone and rang the emergency services. Nicholas said to Rikki that maybe it was a heart attack. Herman had had one six years ago.

The ambulance arrived and Herman was taken away. In the confusion, Nicholas managed to knock over the coffee cup. Lou Dell called Judge Harkin.

♦

Pynex shares opened high on Monday morning. There was good news coming out of Biloxi, though no one knew the source. All tobacco shares rose in early, heavy trading.

Judge Harkin arrived in court at nine-thirty. He'd been arguing with Rohr and Cable. Cable wanted a new trial after the loss of another juror, but the Judge didn't agree.

Fitch sat in amazement. How do you give someone a heart attack? Was Marlee capable of poisoning a blind man? Thank God she was on his side.

Judge Harkin told the jurors that Herman wasn't in danger. Everyone was very relieved, and Shine Royce took Herman's place. The Judge asked Wendall Rohr to start his closing speech. It went well, lasting forty-eight minutes, and he ended it with some figures. You could value Jacob Wood's life at a million dollars. Add some other damages, and the total sum that the family were due was two million. But there was also the role of punitive damages. How do you punish a company that has $800 million in cash?

He was careful not to suggest a figure.

In response, Durwood Cable took slightly more than half an hour to dismiss the idea that you should give millions to the family of a man who'd smoked for thirty-five years. It was just a means of getting money. He appealed to the jury's sense of fairness, asking them to judge the case on facts not emotions. He had the jury's complete attention.

The Judge told the jury that the case was now for them to

decide. He asked them to select a new foreman, in place of Herman Grimes. As the jury left, Nicholas turned and looked at Fitch. Fitch nodded.

Fitch left the court and went to his office. Marlee phoned.

"Fitch, I have new transfer instructions for the money." She wanted it sent to a bank in Panama City. "You have twenty minutes, Fitch. The jury is eating lunch. If I don't have confirmation by twelve-thirty, then the deal's off and Nicholas will change direction."

Within ten minutes the money was on its way. He received confirmation by fax. At 12:20, Marlee called her banker in Panama, who confirmed receipt of ten million dollars.

Marlee was in a motel room ten kilometers away, with a fax machine. After five minutes, she instructed the same banker to transfer the money to a bank in the Cayman Islands. Nicholas called at twelve-thirty to learn that the money was safe. Marlee went straight to the airport, where a small plane was waiting.

◆

Swanson had waited patiently for Beverly. She'd rung him at 3:30 A.M. Monday morning, obviously drunk, and arranged to meet him at 7 A.M. in the coffee shop. She was four hours late, and looked drugged, but Swanson could have kissed her.

"Have you got the money?" There was no doubt what the money would be spent on.

"Yes, but tell me about Claire."

Beverly gave him the information she'd got from Phoebe. "Now give me the money," she said.

Swanson handed her the envelope. "Thanks," he said, and disappeared.

He finally reached Fitch on the phone just after one. By then, Swanson was on his way to Missouri.

Chapter 14   The Verdict

In the jury room, they were ready to do what they'd been dreaming about all month. They took their places and stared at the empty seat at the end of the table, the one that Herman had occupied.

"Guess we need a new foreman," said Jerry.

"And I think it should be Nicholas," Millie added quickly. There wasn't any doubt about who the new foreman would be. No one else wanted the job, and Nicholas seemed to know as much about the trial as the lawyers.

Nicholas started. "Judge Harkin wants us to consider all the evidence, including the reports, before we start voting," he said.

"I'm ready to vote now," said Lonnie Shaver.

"Not so fast," said Nicholas. "This is a very complicated case and it would be wrong to rush things."

"We're not going to read all that stuff are we?" asked Sylvia.

"I have an idea," said Nicholas. "We'll each take a report, read it fast, and then make a summary for everyone else."

They started work.

◆

Marlee's flight from Biloxi to George Town, Grand Cayman, took ninety minutes. She went through customs with a new passport which showed her to be Lane MacRoland, a Canadian. She took a taxi to the Royal Swiss Trust bank. The tropical air was warm, but Marlee hardly noticed.

She was greeted by a receptionist and within minutes had met a young man named Marcus. They'd spoken many times on the phone. The money had arrived, he told her. In his office, a secretary bought coffee and Marlee ordered a sandwich.

Pynex shares were still strong when Marlee made her first trade. She sold 50,000 shares in Pynex at seventy-nine dollars, using a system which was popular with experienced investors. If the price of shares was going to fall, trading rules allowed them to be sold first at the higher price, then purchased later at the lower one. With ten million dollars in cash, Marlee would be allowed to sell approximately twenty million dollars' worth of shares. Later, she'd buy them back, and if their price had fallen, she'd make a profit on the difference in price.

Marcus confirmed the trade, and Marlee then sold shares in two other Big Four companies, and then more in Pynex. She paused and instructed Marcus to watch Pynex closely. She'd just sold 110,000 shares, and was worried about the effect on Wall Street.

"I think it's safe now," said Marcus, who'd been watching the share price closely for two weeks.

"Sell 50,000 more," she said, without hesitation. She was very calm.

Marcus's heart missed a beat, then he completed the trade. "That's approximately twenty-two million dollars, Ms. MacRoland. I think we should stop. More sales will need approval from my superior. One question. When do you anticipate movement on these shares?"

"Tomorrow, early. If you want your other clients to think you're really smart, then you should suggest that they follow my example."

Marcus sent for a company car to take Marlee to her hotel.

♦

Marlee's present seemed under control, but her past was being discovered. At the University of Missouri, records were found of a Dr. Evelyn Y. Brant. She'd died in 1987, age fifty-six, and left everything to her daughter, Gabrielle, age twenty-one. Gabrielle had received nearly $200,000. On the death certificate it stated that Dr. Brant had died of lung cancer.

By the time Fitch was told this, they knew more. Dr. Brant's husband, Dr. Peter Brant, had died in 1981 at the age of fifty-two, leaving everything to his dear wife Evelyn and his daughter, Gabrielle. He'd also died of lung cancer.

Fitch took the telephone call from Swanson alone, with the door locked. At first, he was too shocked to react. Both of Marlee's parents had died of lung cancer! He wrote it down on a yellow pad as if he could analyze it, as if he could somehow make it fit in with her promise to deliver a verdict.

He closed his eyes and rubbed his head. He must stay calm. There was nothing he could do to stop the jury's discussions. They were in there, with deputies by the door. Fitch made a list of possible things he could do, all of which would be dangerous, illegal, and would fail.

He slowly rose to his feet, and took the glass lamp in both hands. Konrad and Pang were standing outside and heard a crash as the lamp hit the wall. Fitch shouted something about "the money," then the desk hit the wall.

"Find the girl!" he screamed. "Find the girl!"

♦

After the period of forced concentration, Nicholas decided that some debate was needed. He started by summarizing a report on the state of Jacob Wood's lungs. His audience was bored.

"I have an idea," Rikki Coleman said. "Let's see if we can all agree that cigarettes cause lung cancer."

"Fine with me," said Nicholas. "Raise your hands if you believe that cigarettes cause lung cancer." Twelve hands went up in the air.

"Who thinks nicotine is addictive?" Another yes vote.

"Let's keep united, folks," Nicholas said. "It's really important that we walk out of here voting the same way." Most of the jurors had heard him say this before. The legal reasons weren't clear, but they believed him anyway. They continued to work through the reports. They left the room to smoke and to stretch. Lou Dell and two deputies guarded the door.

After another juror had summarized a report on the contents of cigarette smoke, Lonnie Shaver spoke.

"I thought we'd decided that cigarette smoke was harmful." He looked at Nicholas. "I say we get on with the voting. I'll go first." He took a deep breath and everyone turned to watch him. "My position is easy. I believe cigarettes kill. That's why I leave them alone. Nobody can force you to smoke, but if you do, you'll suffer the consequences. Don't smoke for thirty years, and then expect me to make you rich . . . These crazy lawsuits need to be stopped."

"Do you know when I started smoking?" said Angel Weese. "I remember the exact day. I was thirteen, and I saw this really good-looking guy, all smiles, perfect teeth, with a beautiful girl on his arm, and a cigarette in one hand. 'What great fun,' I thought. 'There's the good life.' So I went home, got my money, and bought a pack of cigarettes. Don't try and tell me anyone can give up. I'm addicted."

Lonnie said nothing. The arguments continued, then the jury returned to their reading. At five o'clock, Judge Harkin called them back. "You've had the case for five hours. I'd like to know if you're making progress."

Nicholas stood up. "I think so, Your Honor. We're determined to finish and have a verdict sometime tonight."

"Wonderful. Thank you. Dinner is on the way. I'll be in my chambers if you need me."

♦

Dinner was over at six-thirty, and the jury agreed to vote.

"Are you willing to hold Pynex responsible for the death of Jacob Wood?" asked Nicholas. Four jurors voted yes, four no, the rest weren't sure.

"I think it's time for you to say what you think," Lonnie said to Nicholas.

"OK," he said. He'd practiced this speech, and spoke very persuasively. "I'm certain that cigarettes are dangerous—they kill 400,000 people a year and they are full of nicotine. I think cigarettes killed Jacob Wood and I am also certain that tobacco companies lie and cheat and do everything in their power to persuade kids to smoke. They are selfish and greedy and should be punished."

Rikki Coleman and Millie Dupree felt like clapping.

"You want punitive damages?" asked Jerry.

"The verdict means nothing if it's not significant. It has to be huge."

They went round the table again—seven for the plaintiff, three for the defense.

"How much money do you have in mind for Celeste Wood?" asked Rikki.

"A billion dollars." Mouths fell open.

"That's ridiculous," said Lonnie. At that moment, most of the other jurors agreed. The discussions continued. Finally, they agreed ten votes to two that Celeste Wood should receive two million dollars in actual damages. After the mention of a billion dollars, two million seemed a very small amount. Again, they voted ten to two for punitive damages. "Any idea of how much?" asked Nicholas.

"I have an idea," said Jerry. "Get everyone to write down their amounts on a piece of paper, then add them up and divide by ten. That way we'll see what the average is."

The jurors quickly wrote their numbers on pieces of paper. Nicholas slowly unfolded each piece of paper and called the numbers out to Millie, who wrote them down. One billion, one million, fifty million, ten million, one billion, one million, five million, five hundred million, one billion, and two million.

Millie did the math. "The average is three hundred fifty-six million, nine hundred thousand."

Lonnie jumped to his feet. "You're crazy," he said and left the room, banging the door behind him.

Another juror looked shocked. "I can't do this. I'm retired, OK. I have enough money, but I can't understand these figures."

"These numbers are real," Nicholas said, "and the company is very rich. It has eight hundred million in cash. We've got to think big, or they won't take any notice."

"What will happen to the tobacco industry if we bring back a big verdict like this?" asked Angel.

"There'll be a lot of action. The industry will have to examine their advertising plans again. They'll go to the government and demand special laws, but I suspect they'll get less and less help. The industry will never be the same," Nicholas answered. "We need to decide on an amount, folks, if we want to go home."

"I have an idea," said Jerry. "Let's take it up to four hundred million, half their cash."

"Count the votes," said Nicholas. Nine hands went up. He filled in the verdict form and made everyone sign it. Lonnie returned.

"We've come to a verdict, Lonnie."

"What a surprise. How much?"

"Two million dollars, and four hundred million dollars. Care to join us?"

"Hell, no," answered Lonnie.

Nicholas walked to the door and asked Lou Dell to inform Judge Harkin that his jury was ready.

While they waited, Lonnie whispered to Nicholas, "Is there any way I can say that I didn't agree?" He was more nervous than angry.

"Sure, don't worry. The Judge will ask each one if this is our verdict. When he asks you, make sure everyone knows you don't agree with it."

"Thanks."

Chapter 15   Fitch's Surprise

Lou Dell delivered a note from Nicholas to the Judge. In it, Nicholas asked for a deputy to accompany him from the courthouse as soon as the trial was finished. He said he was scared.

The Judge gave the necessary instructions, and then went into the courtroom. The atmosphere was full of anticipation. Lawyers were walking around, nervous and wild-eyed. It was almost eight o'clock.

"I have been informed that the jury has reached a verdict," Harkin said loudly. "Please bring in the jury."

They came in looking serious. Lou Dell took the verdict form from Nicholas and handed it to the Judge. His face showed no reaction to the extraordinary news he was holding. He was very shocked, but there was nothing he could do. It was technically correct. There would be action to reduce it later on, but he couldn't do anything now. He gave it back to Lou Dell, who asked Nicholas to read it.

"We, the jury, find in favor of the plaintiff, Celeste Wood, and grant her damages of two million dollars."

Wendall Rohr and his lawyers breathed a huge sigh of relief. They'd just made history.

But the jury wasn't finished. "And we, the jury, find in favor of the plaintiff, Celeste Wood, and grant punitive damages of four hundred million dollars."

Cable sank down into his chair as if he'd been shot. The other defense lawyers stared at the jury box, mouths open, eyes wide in total disbelief. "Oh my God!" one of them said.

Rohr was all smiles as he put his arm around Celeste Wood, who'd started crying. The other lawyers with Rohr congratulated each other. Oh, the thrill of victory, the thought of sharing 40 percent of this verdict.

"Now, ladies and gentlemen of the jury," Judge Harkin said. "I am going to ask each of you individually if you voted in favor of this verdict."

"I did," answered Nicholas Easter and six others. When it came to Lonnie, he said loudly, "No, your Honor, I did not. I disagree with this verdict entirely." Two more jurors said they hadn't voted for the verdict, but the final two, Sylvia and Jerry, stated they'd supported it. The vote was nine to three.

Nicholas was extremely worried that Fitch wasn't in court. How much did he now know? Nicholas wanted to get out of the courtroom and leave town. The Judge thanked the jury and told them that they couldn't tell anyone about the discussions they'd had. They were dismissed.

Fitch was watching from the viewing room in his office. He was alone; all the jury consultants had been dismissed. He'd discussed what he could do with Swanson. They could kidnap Easter, but he wouldn't talk and they'd go to jail for it. They decided to follow him, hoping he'd lead them to Marlee. But what could they do if they found her? They couldn't report her to the police.

Fitch was trapped whatever he did.

Nicholas left court quickly without saying goodbye to anyone. At the back entrance, the Sheriff was waiting for him in his car. "Judge said you needed some help." Nicholas directed him to a large apartment building north of town and got out, thanking the Sheriff. He then got in a new rental car that Marlee had left there two days ago and drove to Hattiesburg, where a private plane was waiting. He arrived in George Town with new Canadian papers. Marlee met him at the airport. They kissed.

"Have you heard?" he asked.

"Sure, it's all over CNN,"★ she said. "Was that the best you could do?" she asked with a laugh. They kissed again.

They went to the beach and sat in the sand alone as the waves washed across their feet. What a moment it was. Their four-year operation was over. Their plans had finally worked, perfectly.

♦

Marlee went alone to the Royal Swiss Trust bank the following day. Marcus greeted her in his office.

"Your trade in Pynex shares seems to have been extremely successful. I've been on the phone to New York, and things are really confused. The verdict has surprised everyone. Except you, I guess." There were so many questions he wanted to ask, but he knew there would be no answers. "They might stop trading for a day or two." He looked at his computer, and spoke to someone in New York. "They're offering Pynex shares at fifty dollars." Two minutes passed. His eyes never left the computer screen. "They're at forty-five now. Yes or no?"

"No. What about the others?" Marcus's fingers danced across the keyboard. "The entire tobacco industry is down."

"Check Pynex again," Marlee said.

"Still falling. Forty-two, with a few small buyers."

"Buy 20,000 shares at forty-two."

A few seconds passed before he said, "Confirmed." The Marlee–Nicholas team had just made seven hundred and forty thousand dollars, less the bank's fees. She went on buying slowly. The quick kill was happening. She'd planned this very carefully, and she'd never have another opportunity.

★ CNN: an American TV news channel.

94

A few minutes before noon, with the market still very upset, she'd finished. Marcus wiped his forehead.

"Not a bad morning, Ms. MacRoland. You've made over eight million dollars, less fees."

"I want the money transferred to a bank in Zurich." She handed him written instructions. "Immediately, please."

She packed quickly. Then Nicholas and Marlee flew first class to Miami, where they waited two hours and flew on to Amsterdam. They watched the news in the plane. Wall Street was going round in circles. Experts were speaking everywhere. Judge Harkin had no comment. Cable couldn't be found, but Rohr finally came out of his office and took the credit for the victory.

From Amsterdam they flew to Geneva, where they rented a hotel apartment for a month.

♦

Fitch left Biloxi three days after the verdict. His future as director of The Fund was in doubt, but his firm had plenty of other work. Not as well paid as The Fund, however.

A week after the verdict, he met with Luther Vandemeer and D. Martin Jankle in New York, and confessed every detail of his deal with Marlee. It wasn't a pleasant meeting.

He also discussed with other New York lawyers the best way of attacking the verdict. The fact that Easter had disappeared immediately was suspicious. Herman Grimes had agreed to release his medical records, which showed that he'd been fit and healthy until that morning. He remembered an odd taste to his coffee, then he was on the floor. Colonel Frank Herrera had already given a sworn statement which said that the magazines under his bed weren't his. The mystery surrounding the verdict increased.

The New York lawyers didn't know about the Marlee deal. They never would.

Cable was planning to ask permission to interview all the

jurors, an idea that Judge Harkin seemed to like. How else could they find out what had happened in there? Lonnie Shaver was particularly anxious to talk. He'd received his promotion and was ready to defend American business.

The appeal would be long and difficult.

Rohr's future was filled with opportunity. Extra staff were employed just to answer the phone calls from other lawyers and possible victims. Wall Street seemed more sympathetic to Rohr than to the tobacco industry. The share prices stayed low. Antismoking groups openly predicted the bankruptcy and eventual death of the tobacco industry.

◆

Six weeks after he left Biloxi, Fitch was eating lunch alone in a tiny Indian restaurant near Dupont Circle in Washington. It was snowing outside.

She appeared from nowhere. "Hi, Fitch," she said, and he dropped his spoon.

"What are you doing here?" he said, without moving his lips. He remembered how pretty she was. Her hair seemed shorter.

"Just came to say hello."

"You've said it."

"And the money is being returned to you, as we speak. I'm transferring it back to your account. All ten million dollars, Fitch."

He could think of no quick response. He was looking at the lovely face of the only person who'd ever beaten him. "How kind of you," he said.

"I started to give it away, you know, to some of the antismoking groups, but we decided against it."

"How's Nicholas?"

"He's fine."

"Why are you returning it?"

"It's not mine. I never planned to keep the money. I just wanted to borrow it. Tell me, Fitch, did you find Gabrielle?"

"Yes, we did."

"And her parents?"

"We know where they are."

"Does it make more sense now?"

"It makes more sense, yes."

"They were both wonderful people. They were intelligent and energetic and loved life. They both got addicted to cigarettes in college and I watched them fight their habit until they died. They died terrible deaths, Fitch. I was their only child. My mother died at home on the sofa because she couldn't walk to her bedroom." She paused, but her eyes were surprisingly clear. It must have been sad, but Fitch could feel no sympathy.

"When did you start this operation?"

"Graduate school. I studied finance, thought about law, and then I dated a lawyer and heard stories of tobacco litigation. The idea grew."

"An amazing idea."

"Thanks, Fitch. From you, that's a nice thing to hear."

"Are you finished with us?"

"No. We'll watch the appeal closely, and if your lawyers go too far attacking the verdict, then I've got copies of the bank transfers. Be careful, Fitch. We're proud of that verdict, and we're always watching. And remember, Fitch, next time you go to trial, we'll be there."

ACTIVITIES

Chapters 1–3

Before you read

1 Read the Introduction and answer these questions.

    a What are most John Grisham stories about?

    b Why are his stories successful?

2 Look at the Word List at the back of the book. Which words

    a are for people?

    b refer to trials and courtrooms?

3 Discuss these questions with another student.

    a At a trial in your country, who decides

        • whether a defendant is innocent or guilty?

        • the punishment after a guilty verdict?

    b What are the advantages and disadvantages of a jury system?

    c Should tobacco companies be legally responsible for people who die from smoking-related diseases? Why (not)?

While you read

4 Complete the sentences below with the following names.

Durwood Cable   Nicholas Easter   Rankin Fitch

Herman Grimes   Colonel Frank Herrera   D. Martin Jankle

Marlee   Wendall Rohr   Lonnie Shaver   Celeste Wood

    a .... manages The Fund.

    b ....'s company is involved in a lawsuit.

    c .... is suing the tobacco company.

    d .... is the plaintiff's main lawyer.

    e .... is a mysterious juror.

    f .... is the main lawyer for the defense.

    g .... becomes the foreman of the jury.

    h .... sends a mysterious message to the tobacco companies' fund manager.

    i The tobacco companies plan to put pressure on .... to support them.

    j .... is reported to the judge by another juror.

5 How are these important in this part of the story?

    a smoking

    b Biloxi

    c the Cimmino tobacco case

    d Mary Mahoney's restaurant

    e video films

    f Nicholas Easter's clothes

    g secret cameras

    h Hadley Brothers grocery company

    i the October 12 issue of *Sports Illustrated*

6 Work with another student and have this conversation between Wendall Rohr and Rankin Fitch before the court case.

    Student A: You are Wendall Rohr. You think that you will win the case against Pynex. Tell Rankin Fitch why.

    Student B: You are Rankin Fitch. You think that Pynex will win the case. Tell Wendall Rohr why.

7 "This wasn't an ordinary tobacco case …" Discuss why both sides are so anxious to win.

Chapters 4–6

8 How might Fitch and his team attempt to influence the jury's verdict? What could the judge do to try and stop them?

While you read

9 Tick (✓) the correct ending to each sentence.

    a Lonnie Shaver is offered

        1) a better-paid job in a major tobacco company.   .....

        2) the possibility of promotion.   .....

    b Doyle goes to Chicago because Rankin Fitch

        1) cannot use him any more.   .....

        2) needs him to find out more information about Nicholas Easter.   .....

    c The jury go on strike in the jury room because they do not want

        1) their bags to be searched.   .....

        2) to be sequestered.   .....

d In the Siesta Motel, the jurors go on strike because
they are not allowed to
   1) watch movies. .....
   2) use telephones. .....

e Fitch wants Marlee to eat or drink so that he
   1) has more time to ask her questions. .....
   2) can collect her fingerprints. .....

f Lawrence Krigler's evidence helps
   1) the plaintiff. .....
   2) Pynex. .....

g Wendall Rohr
   1) protects a witness who is in danger. .....
   2) secretly tries to influence a juror. .....

h Hoppy Dupree is
   1) a member of the jury. .....
   2) married to a member of the jury. .....

i Fitch discovers that Nicholas Easter has
   1) been on the jury in previous tobacco trials. .....
   2) used other names. .....

After you read

10 How do these people feel, and why?
   a Wendall Rohr, about Marlee's fax
   b Judge Harkin, Rankin Fitch, and Wendall Rohr, when the jurors
give the Pledge of Allegiance
   c Lonnie Shaver, about entering the smart country club
   d Lonnie Shaver, after talking to Taunton
   e Rankin Fitch, about Rikki Coleman
   f the jurors, after they move into the Siesta Motel
   g Lawrence Krigler, about Pynex
   h Pynex, about Lawrence Krigler
   i Hoppy Dupree, after talking to Todd Ringwald
   j Hoppy Dupree, after talking to Jimmy Hull Moke

11 Discuss these questions with another student.
   a What is the connection between the Stillwater Bay Development
and the lawsuit against Pynex?

b Is Judge Harkin good at his job? Why (not)?

c Why does Marlee keep contacting Rankin Fitch? What is her plan?

Chapters 7–9

Before you read

12 Who is more confident at this point in the trial—Rankin Fitch or Wendall Rohr? Why?

While you read

13 Are these sentences true (✓) or false (✗)?

a Jimmy Hull Moke secretly recorded his conversation with Hoppy Dupree. .....

b Rankin Fitch plans the attack on Nicholas Easter's apartment. .....

c Fitch's computer experts find secret information on one of Nicholas Easter's stolen disks. .....

d The conversation with George Cristano depresses Hoppy Dupree. .....

e Leon Robilio's evidence supports the plaintiff's case. .....

f Nicholas Easter failed his law degree exams. .....

g Wendall Rohr wants the trial to end as soon as possible. .....

h Marlee expects Rankin Fitch to pay her before the verdict is announced. .....

i Rankin Fitch attempts to influence Angel Weese's vote. .....

After you read

14 Who is speaking, who to, and why?

a "We know you're not a crook."

b "Make damn sure you don't kill anyone."

c "Make her see that this case is dangerous."

d "I used to make this argument sound good."

e "She should only show it to people she can trust on the jury."

f "One more phone call like that, and you'll never hear my voice again."

101

g "A verdict for him means you have no job."

h "Make sure she knows how important this case is to the plaintiff."

15 Work with another student. You are Rankin Fitch and Durwood Cable. Discuss the following jurors. Which of them are likely to support Pynex, and which of them are likely to support the plaintiff? Why?

Nicholas Easter   Millie Dupree   Lonnie Shaver   Jerry Fernandez
Rikki Coleman   Colonel Frank Herrera   Herman Grimes
Sylvia Taylor-Tatum   Angel Weese

16 Discuss these questions with another student.

a Why does Rankin Fitch have Nicholas Easter's apartment robbed and burned? Is he wise to do this? Why (not)?

b "People should be free to smoke if they want to." Do you agree with this statement? Why (not)?

c According to Leon Robilio, why do tobacco companies "target young kids"? What is done in your country today to stop this happening?

Chapters 10–12

Before you read

17 What will happen when Hoppy Dupree next meets his wife? Why?

While you read

18 In which order do these happen? Number them 1–10.

a Rankin Fitch and Marlee make a deal.   .....

b The FBI stop the scam on Hoppy Dupree.   .....

c The Chief Executive Officer of Pynex gives evidence
in court.   .....

d A juror is unfairly accused of reading unauthorized
material.   .....

e Hoppy Dupree and his wife learn about Rankin
Fitch's scam.   .....

f	Rankin Fitch argues with the main defense lawyer.	.....
g	Millie Dupree asks Nicholas Easter for help.	.....
h	Hoppy Dupree shows his wife false evidence about a witness.	.....
i	Rankin Fitch transfers a large sum of money to a foreign account.	.....
j	One of Rankin Fitch's men meets an old friend of Marlee's.	.....

After you read

19 Find the correct endings, below, to these sentences.

a The Pynex share price drops suddenly because …

b Taunton is in court because …

c Rankin Fitch and Durwood Cable have a tense discussion immediately after …

d Cleve is angry when …

e Millie Dupree is suspicious when …

f The Sheriff goes to the Siesta Motel because …

g Rankin Fitch has mixed feelings when …

h Swanson pretends to be Jeff Kerr because …

i Millie Dupree cries with joy after …

j The Stillwater Bay Development scam fails because …

1) Colonel Frank Herrera is dismissed from the jury.

2) Hoppy produces a copy of a document that he says has been faxed to him.

3) Nicholas Easter talks about Marlee's investigations.

4) Rankin Fitch wants Lonnie Shaver to listen carefully to a witness.

5) an unauthorized magazine has been found in a juror's room.

6) Angel Weese's boyfriend gets too greedy.

7) Wendall Rohr proves that a witness is lying.

8) Millie Dupree talked to Nicholas Easter about her problems.

9) an article about the trial is written in a financial magazine.

10) Rankin Fitch wants information about Marlee.

103

20 Work with another student. Have this conversation between Rankin Fitch and the D. Martin Jankle, the Pynex CEO.

    Student A: You are Rankin Fitch. You want Pynex to send two million dollars to The Fund. Tell Jankle why you need the money, but do not tell him about Marlee.

    Student B: You are Jankle. You do not want to send The Fund any more money. Tell Rankin Fitch why.

21 Discuss these statements with another student. Do you agree with them? Why (not)?

    a "Millie Dupree has a stronger character than her husband."

    b "Napier and Nitchman should have gone to jail."

    c "Rankin Fitch accepts Marlee's demands too easily."

    d "Wendall Rohr is wrong to have offered Derrick Maples money."

Chapters 13–15

Before you read

22 What will the jury's verdict be? Why?

While you read

23 Is Rankin Fitch pleased (P) or displeased (D), do you think,

    a after his conversation with Marlee about the failed scam? .....

    b about meeting the four CEOs at the beach house? .....

    c about Pynex share prices on Monday morning? .....

    d after the lawyers' final speeches? .....

    e when he hears the truth about Marlee's past? .....

    f about the jury's verdict? .....

    g about his meeting with Luther Vandemeer and Martin Jankle in New York? .....

    h after the release of Colonel Frank Herrera's sworn statement? .....

    i after his meeting with Marlee in an Indian restaurant in Washington? .....

After you read

24 Look at your answers to Question 23. Why is Rankin Fitch pleased or displeased about these events and situations?

25 Only one of these sentences is true. Correct the false sentences.

    a Claire Clement, Gabrielle Brant, and Lane MacRoland are all the same person.

    b Rankin Fitch is worried about Lonnie Shaver.

    c The four CEOs are worried about Rankin Fitch because they have never worked with him before.

    d Wendall Rohr would be pleased if he knew that Derrick Maples had been arrested.

    e Nicholas puts tablets in Herman Grimes's coffee because he is afraid that Grimes might vote against the plaintiff.

    f The other jurors agree with all of Nicholas's suggestions.

    g All the jurors vote in favor of the plaintiff apart from Lonnie Shaver.

    h After the verdict, Rankin Fitch plans to kidnap Nicholas.

    i Marlee is more interested in money than in justice.

    j Rankin Fitch hates Marlee.

26 Work with another student. Have this conversation between D. Martin Jankle and Rankin Fitch.

    Student A: You are Jankle. You do not understand how Rankin failed to win the case for you. Ask him what happened.

    Student B: You are Rankin Fitch. Explain how you failed to win the case, but be careful not to mention Marlee.

27 Discuss these questions with another student.

    a Does the story end as you expected? Why (not)?

    b Do you feel sorry for Rankin Fitch? Why (not)?

    c If you were Marlee, would you return Rankin Fitch's money? Why (not)?

Writing

28 Imagine that you are Colonel Herrera. Write a letter to a friend about your experiences as a juror.

29 Imagine that you are Judge Harkin. You think that, in many ways, this has been the strangest trial that you have ever been involved in. Write an article for a national newspaper, explaining why.

30 Imagine that you are an inspector for the Department of Justice. You have received complaints from some people about the behavior of Nicholas Easter as a juror and later as a foreman. You have investigated the complaints and talked to several witnesses. Now write your report.

31 "No one involved in this trial is completely innocent." Do you agree with this statement? Why (not)?

32 Should smoking be completely banned? Why (not)? Write an essay giving both sides of the argument, then finish with your own opinion.

33 Imagine that you are D. Martin Jankle, the Pynex CEO. Write a letter to Rankin Fitch after the verdict, explaining why you no longer want him to manage The Fund.

34 Imagine that you are Durwood Cable. You want to appeal against the verdict. Write a letter to the Department of Justice explaining why.

35 Imagine that you are Rankin Fitch. You are so impressed with Marlee that you would like her to work for you. Write her a letter explaining why.

36 Imagine that you are Marlee. You have just received a letter from Rankin Fitch inviting you to work for him. Write your reply.

37 Imagine that you are the Secretary of State for Public Health. You are not happy about the behavior of tobacco companies in general. You want them to act more honestly in future and to stop targeting young people in their advertisements. Write them a letter explaining your views and making suggestions for improvements in their future practice.

WORD LIST

allegiance (n) loyalty to a country, belief, or leader

authorize (v) to give official permission for something

casino (n) a place where people try to win money by playing games

chambers (n pl) a room in which a judge can consult privately with lawyers, or hear cases that are not going to court

colonel (n) a middle-ranking officer in the army or air force

damages (n pl) money that someone must pay to another person for harming them or their property

fax (n/v) a document that is sent in electronic form down a telephone line and then printed using a special machine

foreman (n) the leader of a jury

goon (n) an informal word for a violent criminal who is paid to frighten or attack people

lawsuit (n) a problem or complaint that someone brings to a court of law

litigation (n) the process of taking a legal case to a court of law

motel (n) a hotel for people traveling by car, with a place for the car near each room

nicotine (n) a dangerous substance in tobacco

plaintiff (n) the person in a court of law who accuses someone else of doing something illegal

pledge (n) a formal, usually public, promise

punitive damages (n pl) money that is paid to another person as a punishment for harming them

real estate (n) property, like houses or land

research (n) the detailed study of a subject, especially to discover new facts or test new ideas

runaway (adj) moving fast and out of control

scam (n) an informal word for a dishonest plan, usually to get money

sequester (v) to isolate or hide away from other people

settle (v) to decide on something; to make an agreement, for example a financial one, that ends an argument

share (n) one of the equal parts into which the ownership of a company is divided

sue (v) to make a legal claim against someone who has harmed you, especially for money

summons (n) an official order to appear in a court of law

supervisor (n) someone who is responsible for a group of workers and makes sure that they do their job properly

testify (v) to make a formal statement of the truth in a court of law

testimony (n) a formal statement of what is true, especially one made in a court of law

v. (prep) a word, short for **versus**, used to show that people are against each other in a court of law

verdict (n) an official decision that is made in a court of law about whether someone is guilty of a crime

The Testament
John Grisham

Nate O'Riley is a powerful Washington lawyer. Returning to work after a long stay in hospital is difficult for Nate. Then he is sent on a journey that takes him from the tense courtrooms of Washington to the dangerous swamps of Brazil. It is a journey that will change his life forever …

The Chamber
John Grisham

The horror of death row is that you die a little each day. The waiting kills you. Seventy-year-old Sam Cayhall is on Mississippi's death row. Sam hates lawyers but his date with the gas chamber is close, and time is running out. Then Adam Hall, a young lawyer arrives. Can he and his secret persuade Sam to accept his help?

A Time to Kill
John Grisham

Ten-year-old Tonya Hailey is attacked and raped by two local men. Carl Lee, Tonya's father, shoots them. Now only his lawyer and friend, Jake Brigance, stands between him and the electric chair. Is there a legal defense for Carl Lee's actions?

There are hundreds of Penguin Readers to choose from – world classics, film adaptations, modern-day crime and adventure, short stories, biographies, American classics, non-fiction, plays ...

For a complete list of all Penguin Readers titles, please contact your local Pearson Longman office or visit our website.

Misery
Stephen King

A story by Stephen King – the master of horror. Paul Sheldon is Annie Wilkes's favourite writer. She loves all his books about Misery Chastain. When Annie finds Paul after a car accident, she takes him home to look after him. The Annie discovers that Paul wants to kill Misery and to write different kinds of book. She is determined to stop him, and Paul becomes her prisoner.

The Beach
Alex Garland

'Close your eyes … imagine idyllic white sands and coral gardens.' Richard arrives in Thailand. He hears about 'the beach', a secret island. It is paradise on earth. He goes there, but paradise soon turns into hell …

The Body
Stephen King

Gordie Lanchance and his three friends are always ready for adventure. When they hear about a dead body in the forest they go to look for it. Then they discover how cruel the world can be.

There are hundreds of Penguin Readers to choose from – world classics, film adaptations, modern-day crime and adventure, short stories, biographies, American classics, non-fiction, plays …

For a complete list of all Penguin Readers titles, please contact your local Pearson Longman office or visit our website.

www.penguinreaders.com

Cry, the Beloved Country
Alan Paton

'When people go to Johannesburg, they do not come back.' Cry, the Beloved Country is the moving story of two families in South Africa – one black and one white – who are brought into violent contact. From a remote valley in Natal, Reverend Kumalo sets off for the city of Johannesburg in search of his younger sister and his son.

Schindler's List
Thomas Keneally

Thomas Keneally's famous novel tells the true story of Oskar Schindler, a businessman who risked his life every day during the Second World War to save as many Jews as possible. Steven Spielberg's film of *Schindler's List* won seven Oscars, including Best Picture and Best Director.

The Brethren
John Grisham

Three former judges are in prison. They call themselves the Brethren and organize a pen-pal scam. The money is pouring in. But then the Brethren contact the wrong pen-pal – a powerful man with dangerous friends.

There are hundreds of Penguin Readers to choose from – world classics, film adaptations, modern-day crime and adventure, short stories, biographies, American classics, non-fiction, plays ...

For a complete list of all Penguin Readers titles, please contact your local Pearson Longman office or visit our website.

www.penguinreaders.com

Longman Dictionaries

Express yourself with confidence!

Longman has led the way in ELT dictionaries since 1935. We constantly talk to students and teachers around the world to find out what they need from a learner's dictionary.

Why choose a Longman dictionary?

Easy to understand

Longman invented the Defining Vocabulary – 2000 of the most common words which are used to write the definitions in our dictionaries. So Longman definitions are always clear and easy to understand.

Real, natural English

All Longman dictionaries contain natural examples taken from real-life that help explain the meaning of a word and show you how to use it in context.

Avoid common mistakes

Longman dictionaries are written specially for learners, and we make sure that you get all the help you need to avoid common mistakes. We analyse typical learners' mistakes and include notes on how to avoid them.

Innovative CD-ROMs

Longman are leaders in dictionary CD-ROM innovation. Did you know that a dictionary CD-ROM includes features to help improve your pronunciation, help you practice for exams and improve your writing skills?

For details of all Longman dictionaries, and to choose the one that's right for you, visit our website:

www.longman.com/dictionaries